THE MEDUSA RITUAL

PIERCE MOSTYN PARANORMAL INVESTIGATIONS
BOOK 5

C W HAWES

For Jack Koblas, who's gone but not forgotten

ENTER THE IMAGINATIVE WORLD OF CW HAWES

Enter my world. A world of terror on a cosmic scale. Just click, tap, or scan the QR code below.

Fear is the most primal of human emotions. And fear of the unknown is the most terrifying of all fears.

If you are new to the Pierce Mostyn Paranormal

Investigations series, then *The Medusa Ritual* is an excellent entry point into the series and into my world.

In addition to my Pierce Mostyn Paranormal Investigations books, I've written short stories set in the world of the macabre and arcane. Many of which are only available to folks on my mailing list.

So just click, tap, or scan the QR code to enter my world of terror and the macabre. You will get a free copy of *The Feeder* and you'll get my monthly email of news and curated contact. Terror awaits!

PROLOGUE

THE SMALL FIRE crackled and sent whiffs of smoke drifting lazily into the June night sky spread out over Los Angeles.

No burning was allowed, but he'd be damned if he was going to eat the hot dogs cold. Besides, what could possibly catch on fire in this concrete jungle? Nothing but concrete, brick, asphalt, steel, and glass as far as you could see.

Nope. Nothing burnable except the scraps of wood he'd found in the abandoned warehouse. Damn politicians. Always making life difficult. As if it wasn't difficult enough already.

He took a stick and maneuvered the small can of baked beans out of the fire. He stuck a spoon into the bubbling contents and lifted out a spoonful. He blew on the beans until they were cool enough to put in his mouth.

He chewed and swallowed, while holding a hot dog skewered on a long stick, over the fire. With his other hand, he scooped up a spoonful of beans. He blew on them and then put the spoon in his mouth.

Something was preying on homeless people again. He'd heard that at the mission this morning from One-Tooth Bill and Skinny Sue. Sitting there at the long table eating oatmeal with raisins. God, he hated raisins.

They'd said three nights ago the loner guy everyone called Dopey hadn't shown up for supper at the mission and no one's seen him since. And two nights before that, Needle Nancy vanished. Last night, the guy everyone called John Donne, because he was always quoting poetry, was with Luke, Smitty, and Travis. John went off to take a leak. They heard him scream and when they found him, he was curled into a ball and petrified.

He'd asked, "Petrified? Like scared?"

And Skinny Sue, her eyes all big, and not from dope, said, "No. Like in stone."

He'd let out a laugh and told One-Tooth and Skinny those three'd been drinkin' too much Doc Tichner's.

However, when they left, One-Tooth had looked him in the eye, all serious like, and told him to be careful. To be polite, he'd told One-Tooth he would.

He shook his head. If you're going to drink, at least find some real booze. He'd given it up, himself. Getting the crap beat out of him and robbed had been incentive enough. Besides, he had to panhandle extra hard to get enough money for booze. And he was sick and tired of panhandling.

He'd saved up enough so he could get himself a harmonica. He was pretty doggone good at the instrument.

He'd play for his supper, as it were. It had to be better than standing in the hot sun at intersections all day long trying to get money out of stingy drivers sitting in their air-conditioned Beemers.

The hot dog was done. He blew on it and took a bite off the end.

What was that? He cocked his head and listened again. There it was. A shoe stepping on some grit on the pavement.

"Who's there?" he called out. "I hear ya. Don't pretend ya ain't there."

He heard the shoe once again stepping on grit, rubbing it against the concrete.

"What do you want? I don't have nothin' but some beans and hot dogs. I'll share."

There, at the edge of the firelight, he could see a shape.

"I'll share if you're hungry." He stood. "I don't got nothin'. Just some food."

Into the light stepped a woman. She had a beautiful face and then his eyes took in the rest of her. He screamed.

At the same time he felt himself becoming stiff. It was hard to breathe. No. It wasn't hard to breathe, he couldn't breathe. Couldn't breathe at all. His chest. It didn't move. And his eyes. Everything was disappearing. In a moment, the light from the fire vanished into the blackness of eternal night.

1

_____

AN EERIE, high-pitched piping came from the clearing in the woods. Filtering through the trees was an orange-colored iridescence.

We found it, Mostyn Pierce, Helene Dubreuil's words appeared in Special Agent in Charge Pierce Mostyn's mind.

He gave her a hand signal indicating he'd received her thought, and for a moment thought how much easier his job had become due to Helene's special abilities.

He whispered into his headset, "Dotty, do you hear the piping and see the glow?"

"I'm not deaf and blind, Mostyn."

"Good. I want you and NicAskill to move down the hill and flank the thing from the east."

"Got it," Dr. Dotty Kemper replied, who was one of the world's top forensic anthropologists. She also knew her way around a weapon or two.

"Do you copy, Jones?" Mostyn asked.

"Yep," Special Agent DC Jones replied. "You want Doc Petrie and I to move in from the west, I take it."

"I do."

"On it, Boss."

"Baker here, Mostyn. Dr. Stoppen and I will hold the entrance to the ravine so the thing doesn't escape. Unless you have other plans for us."

"No, I don't. Hold the entrance to the ravine, Willie Lee." Mostyn paused a moment before continuing. "Listen up, everyone. Helene and I will attempt to make the capture. We're moving out now."

He shouldered the bag of transmitters for the Electronic Confinement Array. Helene carried the activation device. She held Mostyn's hand and dematerialized them both.

The cloud of atoms that was Mostyn and Helene carefully moved through the woods. No quick or sudden movements. Mostyn wanted to play it safe, because Helene wasn't sure if being in a dematerialized state rendered them invisible to the thing they were after or not.

At the same time, Dotty Kemper and Special Agent Kymbra NicAskill moved into position on the east side of the clearing, while DC Jones and Dr. Winifred Petrie moved into position on the west.

The closer Mostyn and Helene moved towards the clearing, the louder the piping and the brighter the orange glow became. In addition, Mostyn began to smell a putridly rancid odor wafting on the light breeze. It took all of his willpower to keep his stomach from heaving out his hastily eaten lunch.

In his ear, Mostyn heard Kemper's voice, "My God,

what is that stench?" Focused on the task at hand, Mostyn ignored her.

Helene's voice sounded in his mind. *We are almost at the edge of the clearing.*

Mostyn sent his thoughts back to her. *We'll plant the first transmitter directly ahead, and then move around the creature clockwise.*

Yes, Mostyn Pierce.

They broke into the clearing. Before them was a giant, orange spheroid object. It's surface pockmarked with what appeared to be craters. Mostyn thought the thing looked like an orange moon.

In his mind, Mostyn heard Helene gasp. *It's my Lord—*

Focus, Helene! Mostyn thought.

It was, however, too late. Helene's concentration broke and they flickered back to visibility. In that instant, an arm of orange goo shot out towards them. Mostyn pushed Helene to his left and dived to his right. The arm of goo passed between them, engulfed a tree and withdrew, ripping the tree out of the ground. When the tree made contact with the surface of the sphere, it vanished.

Another orange tentacle shot out towards Mostyn, who rolled out of the way. The tentacle withdrew, grass and rocks stuck to its surface.

Mostyn was headed for the tree line when a scream blasted through his headset. He turned and saw Helene, who'd been snared by one of the thing's protoplasmic tentacles, being pulled towards the monster.

NicAskill's voice blasted through Mostyn's headset. "Incoming!" A moment later a bolt of lightning flashed out of the trees, accompanied by a tremendous thunderclap. Mostyn was knocked off his feet by the concussion of the rapid change in air pressure. From the corner of his eye, he saw the lightning bolt strike the monstrosity.

The creature's piping shot up the register until it was almost out of the range of human hearing. Waves of red and black and gray spread across the sphere from where the lightning bolt had struck the thing. The hideously aberrant singularity rose into the air, and again NicAskill's voice was heard to yell, "Incoming!"

The second lightning bolt blasted its way through the trees and struck the now slowly rotating spheroid. The creature dropped back to earth. The weird orange light began flickering and a dark gray began spreading out from the wounds inflicted by NicAskill's weapon.

Mostyn got up on his hands and knees. His eyes swept the clearing, looking for Helene. He spotted her some seventy feet away from him, lying face down.

He started crawling towards her, and was only barely aware of Jones's voice coming over the headset saying, "I got this!" A split second later, a rocket screamed out of the woods, struck the alien looking abomination and a dull whump sounded as the thermite warhead ignited.

The high-pitched piping soared beyond human hearing. From inside the giant spheroid thing, Mostyn saw an ever expanding red glow, and then flames burst out of the unearthly entity like volcanic eruptions.

A scream rent the air. A scream that came from the creature. A scream that was human, all too human. The monstrous obscenity collapsed into a black, burning ooze.

Mostyn jumped to his feet and ran the remaining distance to Helene. He felt for a pulse and found one. She was still alive. He pressed a key on the radio control box. "Sumer Base, come in Sumer Base, over."

"Sumer Base here, Mostyn."

"Target destroyed. We have one casualty. Need emergency evac."

"Roger, Mostyn. Dispatching now. ETA, four minutes."

The other team members arrived. Dotty Kemper knelt next to Mostyn, and held his hand. "She'll be all right, Pierce. She's tougher than all of us."

"I hope so, Dot. I hope so."

"I know so," Dotty replied. "Now we need to collect as much of that thing's remains as we can for the lab. Bardon will be pissed as it is. The least we can do is save the remains."

"Right, Dot." Mostyn stood. "Okay everybody, listen up. We need to collect as much of that goo over there as we can. It's the creature's remains, and the lab will want it." He looked at Dotty.

"I'll stay with her, Pierce."

Mostyn nodded, and followed the rest of his team to what remained of Tommy John MacIlhenney.

2

IN THE HELICOPTER with Mostyn were Helene and the medic keeping watch on her condition, Dr. Dotty Kemper, and Willie Lee Baker, the team's photographer. Mostyn looked at the sedated Helene lying on the bed. She looked peaceful.

He cast a glance at Dotty. She appeared to be asleep, eyes closed. The three of them had an odd relationship. In part... How should he put it? Managed? Managed by Dr. Rafe Bardon, director of the ultra-secret Office of Unidentified Phenomena. Of course, it was he himself who had created the triangle there in K'n-yan in order to save his team. Still, he felt a bit like Jacob being tricked into marrying Leah, when it was Rachel he wanted.

He sighed, leaned his head back against the headrest, and closed his eyes. Rather than sleep, he found his mind going over the mission. They'd had a simple goal: capture the creature known as Tommy John MacIlhenney. He, or better *it*, had been one of several offspring born to Tace

MacIlhenney, a cousin of the infamous Whateley family of Dunwich.

How Tace had come across the ancient book with its blasphemous formulae and rituals, Bardon didn't know. And to make matters worse, Tace and her offspring had vanished. Why she'd left Tommy John with one of the Whateley families was not known either and the OUP might never know, because that particular Whateley family no longer existed. Part of the hell unleashed by Tommy John before his destruction.

Mostyn was pleased the thing had been destroyed. He could never figure out his boss's penchant for trying to capture these abnormalities. If Bardon had his way, the OUP would have the most bizarre zoo in the universe. *Research*, however, was the word his boss used.

Research. Mostyn shook his head and smiled a mirthless smile.

This horror was gone and the one thing Mostyn knew he could count on was that there would be another one waiting for the Office of Unidentified Phenomena to deal with tomorrow. The most secret agency in the world dealing with the most terrifying monsters in the multiverse, all to save an unsuspecting planet from the destruction threatening it.

He felt the helicopter descend, and then the bump of the landing. In a moment the door opened, and a medical team took Helene to a waiting ambulance. Mostyn started following, when an OUP agent intercepted him.

"Sorry Special Agent Mostyn. Dr. Bardon is waiting to meet with you and your team."

"Now?"

"Yes, now."

"What about a shower and cup of coffee?"

"Sorry, sir. Bardon wants to see you now."

Mostyn sighed, and followed the agent to a waiting unmarked black sedan. He looked over at the second helicopter and saw another agent talking to Jones. Mostyn smiled. Jones's very animated gestures meant he was giving the agent hell, but in the end Jones got in the SUV the agent kept pointing to.

Mostyn let Dotty and Baker precede him into the car. Once he got in, the agent closed the door, gave three taps on the roof, and the sedan sped off into the night.

———

The time was late. Well past 11 PM. Dr. Rafe Bardon stood at the front of the conference room, pipe in hand. He was a little round Englishman, and even at such a late hour of the night was impeccably dressed in a dark brown three-piece suit.

Mostyn and his team sat around the table. Helene, however, was at a secret hospital run by the Office of Unidentified Phenomena.

There was no coffee and there were no boxes of doughnuts. A sign Dr. Bardon was not happy.

Bardon puffed on his pipe for a moment before speaking. "We lost a great opportunity today to learn more about The Great Old Ones."

"I'm sorry, sir," Mostyn said.

"It was Ms. Dubreuil and her superstitious worship of these monstrosities bent on destroying us that caused the loss, not anything Special Agent Mostyn failed to do," Dr. Winifred Petrie declared.

"Unfortunately," Bardon replied, "we did not realize Tommy John MacIlhenney would bear such a close resemblance to his father. The mistake is mine."

"Nevertheless, she should have maintained cover," Petrie said. "She could have gotten us all killed."

A look of displeasure crossed Bardon's face. However, all he said was, "Point taken, Dr. Petrie."

Typical, Mostyn thought. Bardon would never blame Helene. She was his fair-haired girl. His ultimate weapon. A prize snatched from K'n-yan, which was also why he wanted her happy. And for Helene, happiness was being with him, Pierce Mostyn. Bardon also wanted him and Dotty Kemper happy. His three best people. Mostyn had great respect for his boss, yet sometimes... Mostyn shook his head.

"Something the matter, Mr. Mostyn?" Bardon asked.

"No, sir," Mostyn replied.

"Do we know who the father was?" Dr. Otto Stoppen asked.

Mostyn was thankful Stoppen's question spared him from further questions, at least for the moment.

Bardon looked at his pipe and put it in his coat pocket. "Preliminary tests of the remains indicate the father was possibly Abholos, the Devourer in the Mist. But our DNA files are incomplete. It's possible the father was Tsathoggua, the greater brother of Abholos."

"Is there any more we can do on this case?" Mostyn asked.

"Yes, there is," Bardon answered. "I have people searching for Ms. MacIlhenney as we speak. She and her hybrid offspring will be found. I want to know how she made contact.

"We are, in addition, in a much better position than those at Dunwich, some ninety years ago, because of the remains you recovered and Mr. Baker's photographs. Our research staff will be kept very busy."

"Thanks goes to Dr. Kemper for the remains, sir," Mostyn said.

"Duly noted," Bardon replied. He looked at Dotty. "Thank you, Dr. Kemper for your quick thinking, which salvaged the operation."

"You're welcome, sir," Dotty said, a big smile on her face.

Bardon gave Dotty a nod, and turned to Mostyn. "As for you and your team, your part on the MacIlhenney case is over. I have another mission for you."

Jones snapped his fingers in protest.

"What is it, Mr. Jones?" Bardon asked.

"We've put in a lot of time on this case, and then without letting us shower or even grab a cup of coffee, you tell us we're through and you're putting us on another case right away."

Mostyn didn't let the smile show on his face, but it was there. Jones always reminded him of a Greek god. He had devastatingly good looks. Right now, though, he looked more like Mars, or Zeus about to throw a thunderbolt.

Bardon was nonplussed. "You do like your paychecks, do you not, Mr. Jones?"

"I do, sir."

"Good. Soon you'll be earning another one," Bardon said. "I needn't remind you that our adversaries, the ones to whom we are nothing, the ones who want our planet for themselves, never sleep. Never take a day off."

"No, sir, they don't. We know that," Mostyn said. "It is, though, as Jones said. We've put a lot of time in on this mission. It would be nice to see it through to the end. I was also hoping to spend some time with Helene."

Dotty Kemper narrowed her eyes at the mention of Helene's name.

"I understand, Mr. Mostyn. However, this new mission is urgent. I need my best people on it." Bardon's tone was apologetic.

"Very well, sir. What do you have for us?" At this point, Mostyn knew there was no use arguing further. They'd been replaced.

Bardon assumed a stance as though he were lecturing at a university. "There are many avenues by which The Great Old Ones may be summoned or awakened. One such avenue consists of resorting to the formulae contained in ancient books of arcane lore, many of which were hand-written. Some of these ancient tomes we have copies of. Others are known to us only by name. And we must always be cognizant of the fact that there are probably others in existence of which we know nothing."

Dotty Kemper raised her hand.

"Yes, Dr. Kemper?"

"What is the basis on which these formulas work?"

"A good question," Bardon said. "The simple answer is magic."

Dotty snorted her disgust. Mostyn, who was sitting next to her, gently touched her arm. She responded by folding her arms across her chest.

"What's the non-simple answer?" she asked.

Bardon smiled. "The non-simple answer is also simple, Dr. Kemper. We don't actually know. That brilliant seer of the future, Arthur C. Clarke, wrote that any technology which is sufficiently advanced is indistinguishable from magic to those not so advanced."

"Muskets to Native Americans," Mostyn said.

"Precisely, Mr. Mostyn," Bardon replied. He took a bent bulldog and tobacco pouch out of his coat pocket, and began filling the pipe. Once the pipe was filled, he continued.

"So, Dr. Kemper, one could say the formulae in these esoteric and eldritch tomes are science operating at a level which we have not yet attained, and therefore appear to us as magic."

Dotty shook her head and muttered, "Science is not magic."

"Perhaps not to you, Dr. Kemper," Bardon replied.

A guilty look crossed Kemper's face. "You weren't supposed to hear that."

Bardon chuckled. "I have excellent hearing, in part due to magic. Or science, if you prefer." He lit his pipe and went on. "Some of these ancient books are well-known. The *Necronomicon*, for example. Others, such as the *Tarsoid*

Psalms and the *Eltdown Shards*, which are actually pottery fragments and not a book, are the domain of specialists."

Jones called out, "What's the point of all this, sir?"

Bardon puffed on his pipe before answering. "The point, Mr. Jones, is this: I have learned that a previously unknown book has come to light and may be used to create, let us say, issues for the Western World."

"And you want us to find the book," Jones said.

"I do," Bardon affirmed.

"That's right up your alley, Stoppen," Jones said.

"Which is why Dr. Stoppen will be on this mission," Bardon said.

Stoppen was an assistant librarian in the OUP's secret library, which had Mostyn wondering about his suitability for field work. But if Bardon wanted him on the team, on the team he was.

"Do we know what this book looks like?" Kemper asked. "And why am I here if you want a book? I'm a forensic anthropologist."

Bardon smiled. "I'll answer your second question first. There is an interesting phenomenon associated with the book, at least we think it is associated with the book, in which your expertise may come in handy. As for what the book looks like, my sources tell me it is apparently a bound codex, with boards that are covered in black leather. The size of the book is approximately five by eight inches, and it is four inches thick. The title of the volume is *Die Unaussprechlichen Riten von Dem dessen Name Nicht Genannt Werden Kann*, which translates to *The Unspeakable Rites of the One Who Cannot be Named*."

Jones rubbed his hands together, and said, "Ooh, spooky."

"Terrifying is more appropriate, Mr. Jones," Bardon replied. "We do not know what *Die Unaussprechlichen Riten* contains. My sources are unsure when the codex was written, or even who the author was. The best guess is that the volume dates from sometime in the thirteenth century, and may actually be a translation of a much older Latin manuscript."

"When do we leave, Dr. Bardon?" Mostyn asked.

"Tomorrow morning. The folder here," Bardon pointed to the brown object on the table, "outlines your mission. The flash drive inside contains the mission details. Any questions?"

No one had any questions for the OUP director.

"Mr. Mostyn, you'll see Jeffries for any special equipment you might need. Good luck to you all."

3

MOSTYN LOOKED out the window of the jet. Next to him, across the narrow isle was Dotty Kemper. In the seats facing him and Dotty were Willie Lee Baker, the mission's photographer, and Dr. Otto Stoppen. Baker and Stoppen were discussing F-stops.

The other team members were in the seats and on the sofa in the back of the jet. Jones and NicAskill were talking about weapons, while Winifred Petrie, a zoologist, and Harbin Hammerschmidt, a chemist, discussed gardening.

Dotty touched Mostyn's arm. "Are you brooding?"

"No."

"I don't think you've said two words since we got into the air."

"I've said at least two dozen."

"Are you worried about Helene?"

"A little."

"The doctor said she'll be fine."

"I know."

"So what else is on your mind?"

"The book. This mission seems too simple."

Dotty let out a throaty laugh. "If you believe anything Bardon gives us is simple, I have a movie studio in Hollywood I can sell you."

Mostyn smiled. "I just might take you up on that offer. Do I get to star in my own movie?"

"Sure, Pierce." She took his hand, brought it to her lips, and kissed it.

"Good thing we'll be landing in twenty minutes," Baker said.

"Shut up, Willie Lee," Dotty shot back.

"Just letting you know so you can get the timing right."

"Go back to your camera talk."

Baker laughed, said, "Sure Dot", and turned back to Dr. Stoppen and their conversation.

Dotty turned to Mostyn. "There'll be plenty of excitement before we even see this damn book Bardon wants. Mark my words."

"I'm sure you're right, Dot."

The pilot's voice sounded over the intercom, announcing they were making their final approach to the Los Angeles airport. After a moment his voice came back on. "And thank you for flying with OUP airlines, where your secrets are common knowledge to us and we don't let you know a damn thing. And, as always, good luck."

"See, Mostyn," Dotty said, "even the pilot knows the score."

———

A black unmarked van picked up the team and their luggage at the plane, and whisked them off to their hotel. Herndon, the accounting wonk, as Mostyn referred to him, had booked everyone into double rooms.

In the lobby, as Mostyn was handing out room assignments, Baker noted, "Herndon's on a money saving kick again." To which Jones replied, "He's always on a money saving kick. What else is new?"

Mostyn chuckled. "At least this time he remembered Dotty and I are together."

"He had to," Dotty replied. "It's simple math. Four rooms or five rooms. Four if you and I are together, five if we're not."

"Just don't do anything I wouldn't do," Baker said.

Jones slapped Baker on the back. "If they do that we're going to be short two people for this mission."

"What do you mean?" Baker protested. "I'm very faithful..." He and Jones went off to find their room, Baker's protests to Jones's insinuations slowly fading with distance.

Petrie shook her head, said, "Men", and headed for the elevator. NicAskill, her roommate, shrugged, and followed.

Mostyn, Kemper, Hammerschmidt, and Stoppen picked up their luggage and made their way to the elevator.

"Do you know how we are going to locate the book?" Stoppen asked.

"Not really," Mostyn replied. "There is an art exhibit tomorrow. Bardon wants us there. His sources are telling him that's the place to begin. And if Dr. Bardon says that's where we start, then that's where we start."

"I don't normally do field work," Stoppen said. "I was just wondering."

"Quite all right, Doctor," Mostyn replied. "Sometimes we don't even have that much to go on."

There was a ding and the elevator door opened. The four got in and rode to their floor in silence.

Exiting the elevator, Hammerschmidt pointed to a sign. "Looks like our room is down this way. Goodnight, then."

Mostyn bade him and Stoppen goodnight, after which, he and Dotty walked down a different corridor to their room.

"Looks like this is it," he said, while swiping the pass card and pushing the door open.

Once inside, Dotty threw her arms around Mostyn and kissed him. "Do you love me, Pierce?"

"You know I do, Dot."

"More than Helene?"

Mostyn held her tight, kissed her, and said, "That's unfair, Dotty. Helene is different."

Dottie pulled away and sat in a chair. "Bardon and his goddamn magic. Sometimes I really hate the guy."

Mostyn kneeled next to her, and took her hands in his. "I love you, Dotty Kemper. You were first in my heart then, and you're first in my heart now."

"But is that you or Bardon talking?"

"I think my lips were moving. Weren't they?"

"They were."

"Maybe we should get some other things moving as well."

She withdrew her hands from his, and placed them on

his cheeks. "Never let me go, Pierce. I don't care what Bardon does. Never let me go."

"I won't, Dot. I promise."

She kissed him. "I'm holding you to that." She stood. "Okay, Mostyn, let's get some other things moving."

Mostyn stood. "You're on, Kemper."

4

———

IN THE MORNING, the team met in one of the hotel's conference rooms. Mostyn ordered in breakfast. Before they all got settled, Jones did a perfunctory sweep to make sure there were no bugs.

"Don't want state secrets getting out," he quipped.

The team engaged in small talk until the breakfast arrived. When the hotel staff departed, Mostyn began the working breakfast meeting.

"Tonight at eight, we'll be going to the James Cortado art exhibit. Pay particular attention to the sculpture. Ask around and see what you can find out about it from the guests."

"What are we looking for specifically?" Winifred Petrie asked.

"I think that will become apparent when you see the sculptures," Mostyn replied.

"What do you want us to find out?" Harbin Hammer-schmidt asked.

"Whatever you can," Mostyn said. "No matter how outlandish or insignificant it seems."

"I still don't understand what all of this has to do with the book," Otto Stoppen said, his face clearly displaying his puzzlement.

"I don't either, Dr. Stoppen," Mostyn replied. "However, Dr. Bardon thinks there is something of value we'll learn at this exhibit that will aid our search."

Stoppen held up his hand. "And if Dr. Bardon says it is so, it is so."

Mostyn smiled. "That's right."

"Is this a formal occasion?" Petrie asked. "Because if it is, I didn't bring anything formal to wear."

"Yes, it's formal," Mostyn replied. "After lunch a team of OUP people will bring the formal attire and get us fitted if we need it."

"I hope they bring us women different dresses," NicAskill said.

"I think you ladies will have a selection to choose from, all based on information from your personnel files," Mostyn said.

"Really?" NicAskill's face took on a look of genuine surprise.

"You'd be amazed at what is in your file," Baker replied.

"Then, again," Jones said, "you probably don't actually want to know."

"Wow," was all NicAskill managed to say.

"If you live long enough, you'll get used to no longer having a private life," Kemper said.

"You aren't helping things," NicAskill replied.

Dotty shrugged. "It's the truth."

Mostyn held up his hand. "Back on topic, folks. You can do what you want for the rest of the morning. Just be back here in this room by one. Because if your clothes need some tailoring we want maximum time for the tailors to make the alterations. Any questions?"

There were none, and Mostyn continued, "Enjoy your breakfast."

After everyone had eaten and departed, Mostyn asked Kemper if she wanted to see the La Brea tar pits.

"How romantic, Mostyn. Why the hell do you want to go *there*?"

"Always wanted to. Ever since I was a kid."

"Never took you for a dinosaur lover."

"Giant mammals, Kemper. Woolly mammoths and such."

"Details, details."

He pulled her to him and kissed her.

Kemper, longing in her eyes, said, "Are we going to do this or see old bones?"

"See old bones. Let's go."

Kemper laughed. "Petrie was right."

"How's that?"

"Men."

————

The gallery was located at the corner of Beverly Boulevard and Fuller Avenue. Mostyn arranged for two limousines to take the team to the gallery. They were posing as wealthy investors and modern art collectors from New York, and, according to Mostyn, had to look the part.

The men were wearing standard black tuxedoes. The dresses the women were wearing, while similar floor length evening wear, were different enough so they couldn't be accused of wearing the same thing.

Dotty's dress was a dark wine red sleeveless satin number that had a scoop to the middle of her back. NicAskill's was a purple A-Line with a sequined halter top. And Dr. Petrie's was black, with lace running along the neckline and making up the cap sleeves.

The team arrived at eight-thirty. The champagne was flowing freely and each team member took a glass. However, Mostyn had warned them there was to be minimal drinking. They were, after all, on duty.

They spread out and began looking at art and making small talk. Mostyn and Kemper made their way to a wall on which hung two rather large paintings.

She whispered to him, "These have to be the ugliest things I've seen in, I don't know, maybe forever?"

Mostyn whispered back, "I've seen worse."

"God."

An obviously overweight man, who wore his tuxedo badly, stood next to Kemper. The man took a drink from his champagne flute. "The angst. So palpable. It resonates in the soul. Don't you think?"

Dotty looked at him. "It's palpable, all right. As palpable as a morning shit."

A look of indignation appeared on the man's face. "Dear me," he said, and walked away rather briskly.

"We're play acting here, Dotty. Please remember that."

"Look, Mostyn—"

Kemper was interrupted by the approach of a tall and slender man. He was dressed in black slacks, a black turtleneck, black shoes and socks, and had longish black hair that he wore combed straight back from his high forehead.

"If you like the paintings, I'll knock off ten percent for the pair." He smiled, showing his brilliant white teeth.

"You're the artist?" Mostyn asked.

The man took a slight bow. "James Cortado at your service."

"The paintings are very interesting, but my wife was actually more interested in seeing the sculpture."

Kemper smiled at Cortado. "We have a corner that I think just the right sculpture would be perfect in."

"Of course. The sculptures are very unique. As one of a kind, as, say, one person is different from another. Follow me."

Cortado led them to a part of the gallery that was partitioned off from the main room with curtains and movable wall partitions.

"The sculptures are here."

"Why do you have them hidden?" Kemper asked.

"They are only for special investors." He paused, and then continued, "I should let you know they are very expensive." He pulled aside the curtain, and motioned with his hand for Mostyn and Kemper to enter.

Kemper looked at Mostyn, who walked into the area containing the sculptures. Kemper followed, and then Cortado walked in.

One look, and Kemper exclaimed, "Oh, my God, they look real!"

Cortado took a small bow. "Thank you."

She looked at a bat, circled around it, and said, "This is amazing."

"Look at this statue, Dot," Mostyn said.

When she saw what Mostyn was looking at, she said, "A person."

"I think you'll want to see this up close." The tone of his voice was such that she knew he thought it very important.

Kemper walked to where Mostyn was standing, and stood next to him. She gasped. "Oh, my..."

Before them was a statue of a woman sitting on the floor. Her hands were raised as if she were warding off an impending blow, and the look on her face was one of sheer terror.

Kemper examined the statue, slowly walking around it. "I've never seen anything so lifelike. How do you do it?"

Cortado smiled. "Trade secret."

Kemper smiled back. "Of course."

"How much?" Mostyn asked.

Mild disgust flitted across Cortado's face. "If you have to ask, you probably can't afford it. I'll send Milt." And Cortado turned and left.

"Guess you put him off," Kemper said.

"I can't help it I'm not rich. I always ask the price if I don't see it."

Kemper replied, "Tsk, tsk. We're pretending to be rich.

Your middle class is showing." And she shook her finger at Mostyn.

"Sorry," he said, dragging out the two syllables.

She bent close and touched the figure. "It feels like stone, but there's so much more detail than I've ever seen on a statue."

She stood just as a man wearing an ice cream suit walked in.

"Hello," he extended his hand to Mostyn, who took it. "I'm Milt Salzman. I'm James's manager." He gave Kemper a bow.

"I'm sorry I insulted the artist," Mostyn began, "but old habits die hard. I was wondering how much the statue cost."

"The bigger pieces are very unique," Salzman said. "We have three human figures, four rats, and the one bat. Half a million for the rats, one mil for the bat, and ten million for the human figures."

"I see," Mostyn said, while taking his phone out of his pocket. He typed on it and returned it to his pocket.

"Was there a particular piece you were interested in?" Salzman asked.

Kemper was looking at the two other human figures. One was a man lying on his side, his face displaying a profound look of horror. The other was also a man who was walking. His face showed surprise, rather than terror.

"Take a look at these, Pierce, dear."

"The rats don't sell well, if I'm honest with you," Salzman said. "I can knock ten percent off the price."

Mostyn's phone chimed. He took it out of his pocket

and looked at the screen. He smiled and returned the phone to his pocket.

"I'll take the woman, the bat at the entrance, and pick out a rat for me." Mostyn handed his card to Salzman. "Call that number and arrange with my people for pick up. I want them tomorrow. Will that be a problem?"

"The show runs for another four days," Salzman said. "We don't let pieces go before the show ends."

"I want them tomorrow, or no sale," Mostyn said.

"Well, uh," Salzman looked at the card. It told him Mostyn was an investor. "Yes, of course, Mr. Mossman. I'll make arrangements with your people first thing in the morning. We will, of course, have to run a credit check. It's standard policy."

"No. Call them now. They'll pick the items up first thing in the morning." Mostyn took out the phone again, tapped on it, and then showed Salzman the screen. "That's my bank account. You can see I have the money in it."

Salzman looked. "Well, yes, but, well, er... This is all highly irregular."

Mostyn shrugged. "Do you want eleven and a half million, minus the ten percent, or not? This isn't a difficult transaction."

There was a gleam in Salzman's eyes. "Mr. Cortado wants his buyers to be happy."

"Good," Mostyn said. "Make me happy."

5
_____

MOSTYN HELD an early morning breakfast meeting to hear what the other team members had discovered and to report his and Dotty's findings. After the coffee had been poured and everyone had taken what they wanted of the pastries, eggs, bacon, hashbrowns, and toast, Mostyn asked Jones and NicAskill to begin.

Jones, a look of disgust on his face, said, "I never saw such shit in all my life."

Petrie chimed in, "Contemporary art is just plain ugly. Like most people."

"Then you've never seen _good_ contemporary art," NicAskill replied.

Petrie waved away NicAskill's comment.

"Check out Lukas Freeborn, or Amy Gibbons, or Helen Cranshaw."

"Never heard of them," Petrie said.

"Then your ignorance is showing." NicAskill replied, a wicked smile on her face.

Mostyn intervened. "We can discuss modern art another time. What did you learn?"

"Sorry, Boss," NicAskill said. "The fat guy that was talking to you and Dr. Kemper? Well, he came over to us after talking to some skinny old woman in a dress right out of the 1930s. Apparently he owns several of Cortado's paintings and thinks the guy is the cat's meow. I finally got him to talk about Cortado instead of just his paintings. Took some doing, but he finally started to tell me what he knew about our artist."

"So what did he say?" Baker asked.

"Apparently Cortado came out of nowhere about five years ago," NicAskill said. "At first he just sold his paintings. Then about a year and a half ago, Salzman joins him and Cortado starts offering sculptures for sale."

"A year and a half ago is when we first heard of *Die Unaussprechlichen Riten von Dem dessen Name Nicht Genannt Werden Kann*," Dr. Stoppen said, the German words rolling fluently off his tongue.

"Which implies there may be a connection between the book, Salzman, and the statues," Mostyn said. "Good. Anything more you two can add? Jones?"

"Nope," Jones replied. "Nicky said it all."

Mostyn mentally shook his head. The Greek god was moving in for his next conquest. He turned to Winifred Petrie. "Dr. Petrie and Dr. Hammerschmidt, what did you two discover?"

Petrie answered, "Apart from a lot of ugly paintings, not much until I saw the sculptures."

Hammerschmidt interrupted. "Most of the people there

had just heard of Cortado. So they didn't actually know much if anything about him. It seems Jeremy Pitkin, the fat guy in the bad tux, has been something of an evangelist for Cortado. He got most of those people to show up."

"The sculptures are something else," Petrie said, taking back the stage. "In my opinion, I don't see how he could have carved them. My nephew has done some sculpture work and has made some lovely pieces, but he has yet to achieve the detail in his work that this Cortado is claiming to have achieved in his. And my nephew's been sculpting for ten years."

"I'm a chemist, not a geologist," Hammerschmidt said, "so recognizing types of stone is not my field. However, I didn't recognize the stone those sculptures were carved from. If, as Winifred's implied, they were carved at all."

"If I had to take a guess," Baker said, "I think the stone was something akin to marble, which will hold very fine detail, but I don't think it was marble and I've never photographed marble statues with *that* much detail."

Mostyn then told the group his and Dotty's findings, as well as the purchase of the sculptures for the lab people to analyze. When he was done, he asked if anyone had any questions.

"Yeah, I do," Jones said. "What's next?"

"I want you all to start nosing around the art community," Mostyn replied. "Find out everything you can on Salzman and Cortado. We should have a report from headquarters this afternoon. But I want the local talk."

"What about the people at the show?" Petrie asked.

"I don't think they'll be helpful, since Dr. Hammerschmidt said most of them hadn't heard of Cortado prior to last night," Mostyn replied. "However, Mr. Pitkin might be persuaded to tell us more. NicAskill, I'd like you to talk to him. You probably know more about modern art than all of us combined."

"Sure thing, Boss."

"And I think you should talk to him alone," Mostyn added. "I think he'll tell you more that way. He seems to like the ladies. After you're done, catch up with Jones." To the group, he said, "The rest of us will take the partners we had last night. I don't think we'll encounter any problems, but I don't want to take any chances. Questions?"

When Mostyn saw that there weren't any, he told the team to move out.

———

Mostyn drove the black sedan out of the hotel garage.

"Where are we going?" Kemper asked.

"I want to start with the Jewish girl's school across the street from the gallery."

"Why?"

"Because it's there."

"For crying out loud, Mostyn. Do you have to be so goddamn cryptic?"

"No."

"Is that all? Shit?"

Mostyn let out a laugh. "Lighten up, Dot."

Dotty Kemper took a deep breath, and exhaled. "Okay,

Mostyn. Will you please tell me why you want to start at the girl's school?"

"As I said, it's there and because the school is there they might know something."

"Okay, I'll buy that."

"Anymore questions, Dr. Kemper?" A smile tugged at Mostyn's lips.

"Not at the moment, Special Agent in Charge Mostyn."

"Good."

There was a pause and then Dotty asked, "Would you like to retire here, Pierce?"

"I don't know. Haven't thought about it. Off hand, I'd say there are too many people. I'd like to go someplace a little quieter."

"Here in southern California?"

"Sure. Someplace off the beaten path."

"Good. I like it here."

Mostyn thought of Helene and wondered if she'd like it in southern California. He loved Dotty, loved her very much. However, if he was honest with himself, he loved Helene too.

There are times, he thought, *when I wish Helene had left us to our fate down there in K'n-yan. Might have been better for all of us.*

"Penny for your thoughts," Dotty said.

"They aren't even worth that," Mostyn replied. "Just focusing on the traffic."

Mostyn threaded the sedan through the crowded west LA streets and soon they were at their destination. He circled the block twice, before finding a place to park.

"You really think they'll know something here?"

"Probably not," Mostyn replied, "but we won't know until we ask."

"You're the boss."

They walked in the front door of a simple structure shaped like a child's building block with several smaller rectangular-shaped cubes attached and encountered a security guard sitting at a desk. "How may I help you?" the man asked.

"I'm Special Agent in Charge Pierce Mostyn of the IRS." Mostyn showed the guard his ID. "And this is Special Agent Dotty Kemper." Kemper showed her ID. "We'd like to talk with the chief administrator."

"That would be Dr. Abraham Katz. Let me phone and see if he's available." The guard made his phone call, spoke to someone named Miriam on the other end, and after a minute he hung up. He looked at Mostyn. "Miriam, Dr. Katz's secretary, will be here momentarily."

Momentarily stretched into seven minutes, before Mostyn and Kemper heard shoes clip-clopping on the terrazzo floor. Miriam was a short, busty woman, with stylish gray hair, and was dressed in a cream pants suit. She walked up to Mostyn and Kemper.

"I'm Miriam Cantor. If you will follow me?" She turned and started walking back the way she came. Mostyn and Kemper followed. When they reached the door to the office, she paused, and said, "Dr. Katz is very busy."

Mostyn replied, "We won't take up any more of his time than is necessary."

Miriam Cantor opened the door and entered the office, the outer portion of the office as it turned out. She walked up to a door, knocked, opened it wide enough to poke her head in, and then pushed the door open, indicating with her hand Mostyn and Kemper should enter.

Mostyn nodded to her and walked through the doorway, followed by Kemper. Miriam closed the door behind them.

Before them a tall, heavyset man stood behind a large walnut desk. His hair was black and partly covered by a black kippah. He wore a black suit, white shirt, and a red tie with tiny navy blue dots.

He walked around his desk, his hand extended to Mostyn. "I'm Abraham Katz. I understand you're with the IRS?"

"That's correct." Mostyn took the doctor's hand and shook it. "I'm Pierce Mostyn."

Dotty extended her hand. "I'm Dotty Kemper."

Dr. Katz took her hand and held it momentarily before letting go. "Please, have a seat." Katz motioning to a sitting area off to the side of the room.

Mostyn and Kemper sat on the couch and Katz sat in one of the tub chairs.

The administrator folded his hands across his stomach. "I hope we haven't missed something in our bookkeeping."

Mostyn smiled. "We aren't here about the school. At least not directly."

The relief was visible on Katz's face.

Dotty smiled. "Unfortunately our presence has an undesirable effect on people. I apologize."

Mostyn continued, "We're actually investigating some of the artists and art galleries and were hoping you could be of help to us."

"How so?" Katz asked.

"We're looking into the gallery across the street," Mostyn explained, "and in particular an artist named James Cortado and his manager Milt Salzman. Have you had any dealings with the studio or the men?"

"Two, maybe three, years ago Mr. Cortado taught a couple classes here. But he didn't work out and we didn't renew his contract."

"Can you tell us what the issue was?" Dotty asked.

"I'd rather not," Katz replied. "His being here ended up posing a problem with the younger girls, and we let him go."

"Can you tell us anything about him?" Mostyn asked.

"Not really. I didn't know him. Principal Kellerman dealt with him. I can give you her number and you can make arrangements to speak with her directly."

"Thank you," Mostyn said, "that would be helpful."

Katz got up, went to his desk, and sat. He opened a drawer, pulled out a sheet of paper, scanned it, then jotted a note. He got up, and walked to Mostyn, giving him the slip of paper.

"That's her number. Tell her I gave it to you."

Mostyn stood, Dotty also. "Thank you, Dr. Katz," Mostyn said.

"You're welcome. Miriam will show you out."

When they were on the sidewalk, Dotty said, "Well, Cortado is as snaky as he looks."

"What do you mean?"

"They booted him because he was being inappropriate with young girls."

"So it seems," Mostyn replied. "And I'm not surprised given that he's on our radar. He's either up to no good or involved with those who are."

"Agreed. So now what?"

"We talk with the gallery owners."

Mostyn started to cross the street, when a car, tires squealing, raced around the corner. He leapt out of the way just as the car swept over the spot where he'd been standing.

"Are you okay?" Dotty nearly screamed the question.

"I am. Looks like we pissed somebody off. The question is, who?"

6

"IT COULD HAVE BEEN AN ACCIDENT," Dotty said.

"Possible. Best keep our eyes and ears open."

The two crossed the street and entered the gallery. The place was rather dark. Not much light entered in from the windows, and the room lighting was diffused. The only areas of bright light were where the paintings and sculptures were located. Mostyn hadn't paid attention to the artwork on the ground floor, when he entered the building the previous night. He now had his chance to rectify that omission.

To Dotty, he said, "Most of this stuff is hideous. Why would anyone want to buy it, let alone display it?"

"Beats me," Dotty replied. "Art's not my thing."

"Hello. May I help you?" a voice called out from a dark corner. After a moment, a body became visible.

"We were wondering if James Cortado was here," Dotty said.

"I'm François, the owner of the gallery." He stood with an expectant air about him.

"I'm Pierce Mossman, and this is Dotty Kemper. We were here last night to see Mr. Cortado's work."

"Oh, yes," François began, "you made a sizable investment."

"Who told you that?" Dotty asked.

"Milt Salzman, his agent. I had to be here at some ungodly hour so your people could pick up the work. God, couldn't they have picked a decent time of day?"

"Sorry to ruin your sleep," Mostyn said. "Is Cortado here?"

"Mr. Cortado is not here, nor is Mr. Salzman. Perhaps I can help you?" Although the tone of his voice indicated the exact opposite.

"Perhaps you can," Mostyn said, as he pulled out his ID and showed it to François. Mostyn enjoyed watching the gallery owner's eyes become like saucers.

"The IRS? Have they done something wrong? I mean, I have the gallery's reputation to think of."

"Can't say," Mostyn answered. "We would, though, like to talk to them. Do you happen to know their addresses?"

"I might have them. Let me check." He disappeared into the dark corner he'd come from.

While the gallery owner was gone, Kemper and Mostyn looked at the paintings, sculptures, and pottery.

"This pot isn't so bad," Mostyn said, "but I'm not spending eight hundred bucks to have it on my desk."

"Skinflint," Dotty said.

"I don't see you buying anything."

"And you won't. At least here you won't. Now take me to a gun show and you'd better hold on to your wallet."

"I thought knives were more your thing."

"Nope. They're work tools. Give me a handgun any day. They're fun."

"You're dangerous."

François appeared. "Find anything you like?"

"Not really," Dotty said.

"I'm sorry to hear that," the gallery owner replied. "I have a phone number for Milt Salzman. That's all. Sorry."

"We'll take it," Mostyn said.

"If you're with the IRS, don't you, like, have this information already? I mean, you're the government."

Mostyn smiled. "Can't believe everything you see on TV."

"Is there anything you can tell us about them?" Dotty asked.

"I don't actually know them," François replied.

"Yet your gallery is hosting Cortado's show…" Dotty lifted her hands and shrugged.

"Wait a minute." François shook his head. "No. I have nothing to do with them. All I get is a percentage of their sales in exchange for the space. And they're out of here in a few days."

"What can you tell us about them?" Mostyn asked, then added, "Your cooperation will be noted."

"Cortado blew into town some five years ago with a Goth chick named Delora Youngblood. She was then and still is a better painter than Cortado. I think it's what caused them to split. He just couldn't stand having her always showing him up. Anyway, some time after they split, Salzman shows up, takes Cortado under his wing, and suddenly Cortado is going places. All very mystifying, if you ask me."

"Where does Ms. Youngblood live?" Dotty asked.

"The gallery represents her, so I can get you her address. Hang on."

Once more, François retreated to his dark corner and in a moment was back with a slip of paper that he handed to Dotty. "There's her address and phone. She's a good seller for me. I'd rather you not tell her where you got her address and number. Now, I've cooperated and I have work to do. The gallery doesn't run itself."

Mostyn nodded. "You've been very helpful. Thank you."

"Do you actually make a living at this?" Dotty asked.

"What do you mean? Of course, I do."

"Just wondering," Dotty replied.

She and Mostyn left, had no problem crossing the street, and made their way to the car.

"Let's get something to eat," he said, as he got in.

"I'm game," Dotty replied, and got into the vehicle. While putting on her seatbelt, she said, "Can we make it some place expensive?"

"Herndon will squawk."

"Screw him. I'm not doing fast food."

"Down!" Mostyn yelled.

The window shattered, and a javelin impaled the center console, missing Dotty's leg by an inch.

7

MOSTYN JUMPED out of the car and looked up and down the street. People were beginning to gather and a few were pointing at the car that had a javelin sticking out of its windshield. Mostyn called out to them.

"Anyone see which way the person who did this went?"

The onlookers didn't reply and started moving away, leaving Mostyn muttering about goddamn worthless people not wanting to help an obvious victim.

He asked Dotty to hand him some gloves from the glove box. She opened the compartment and handed him a pair. He put them on and yanked the javelin out of the center console. He opened the back door and tossed the thing in onto the rear seat. He closed the door, got back into the car, and looked at Dotty.

"You okay?" he asked.

"I'm okay. I don't think we're dealing with accidents here."

"That's what it's looking like." He took out his phone

and made a call. When finished he returned the phone to his pocket.

"We're to sit tight while they send a new car and a tow for this one," Dotty said, anticipating Mostyn's comment.

"On the money," he replied.

"So who's found out what?"

"Good question, Dot. Offhand, I'd have to say Cortado or Salzman. Perhaps both. As for what they've discovered, I have no clue."

"It's looking like Cortado was basically a nothing until Salzman showed up and took an interest."

"That's what it's looking like. Which begs the question, is Salzman connected to someone?"

Dotty nodded. "That, or maybe Salzman has the book."

"Maybe he does at that. Those sculptures give a whole new meaning to 'life-like'."

"They do. I've never seen anything like it."

"I thought you weren't into art."

Dotty's voice took on an edge. "I'm not. Doesn't mean I'm an ignoramus."

"Didn't say you were."

"It was implied."

Mostyn held his hands up. "I wasn't implying anything. Geez, Kemper, lighten up. I'm on your side."

"Sorry." She looked out the window. "Say, I thought it was sunny all the time in LA."

"It does rain here."

"Okay, but the sun was shining and there wasn't a cloud in the sky. Now it's completely overcast. Where did the clouds come from?"

"Don't know. It does seem odd."

"And it's getting darker."

Mostyn stepped out of the car and looked up at the sky. The clouds were not only getting darker, they also appeared to be churning as though some unseen giant was whipping them up with a hand mixer.

Kemper joined him. "Something's not quite right, is it?"

"You can say that again."

A black limo pulled up, the doors opened, and four men jumped out. Mostyn reached for his gun and stopped when he saw the machine pistol pointed at him.

The few people that were on the street quickly vanished.

One of the men tried to grab Kemper. Her right fist shot out and connected with his lower jaw. He staggered, and fell. Another man grabbed her hair and shoved the muzzle of his pistol against her neck. Dotty stopped fighting.

The man with the machine pistol, indicated with his hand that Mostyn was to get in the car. Mostyn looked at the mirrored sunglasses on the man, and then got in. Kemper was shoved in after him, and the door was closed.

Kemper tried the handle, but the door was locked. The car began moving in the midday traffic.

Across from Mostyn and Kemper was a man wearing a Chinese mask and a heavily embroidered gold robe. The mask was red and decorated with black, indicating a highly stylized beard and eyebrows. On either side of the masked man, was a young man in a black suit, white shirt, and black tie. The suits were well-tailored and there was no bulge indicating a shoulder holster.

They probably have something other than firearms up their sleeves, Mostyn thought.

He looked at the man with the mask and watched the eyes behind the openings shift to Kemper and then return to him.

"What do you want?" Mostyn asked.

After a moment, the mask spoke. The voice sounded ancient, almost ethereal. "I find it interesting you address *what*, rather than *who* first."

The English bore a British accent. *Hong Kong?* Mostyn thought. He shrugged. "It's obvious you want something, given the theatrics you went through to get us here. So at this point *what* is more important than *who*."

"Very logical, Mr. Mostyn. Or is it Mossman?" When there was no response from Mostyn, the man shrugged his shoulders and went on. "Whatever your name is, what I want is for you to leave Los Angeles. You have your art. Now go. And do not return."

"The last time I checked, this was a free country. I can go where I want, when I want, and leave when I'm ready."

"No, Mr. Mostyn, the illustration is incorrect. You are in a casino and the house suspects you of cheating. You are asked to leave. In reality, you are being thrown out."

"I see. And if I don't want to go?"

"Then, as the enforcers in the casino, I will be forced to either add an incentive or use force."

Mostyn looked at Dotty, and she looked back at him. He nodded, turned to the masked man, and said, "I guess we're staying."

"I'm sorry to hear you say that."

The man reached into his sleeve and withdrew a vial. He unscrewed the top and poured a powder into the palm of his hand.

Pistols appeared in the hands of the young men.

Must've been on the car seat next to them, Mostyn thought.

"Now I must use incentive and force," the masked man said. "Goodbye, Mr. Mostyn. May we never meet again." Holding his hand flat, the masked man blew the powder towards Mostyn and Kemper.

Mostyn tried waving it away and that's the last thing he remembered.

8

———————

MOSTYN OPENED HIS EYES. He didn't move anything except for his eyes. He took in everything he could see without moving his head. The lighting was subdued. The ceiling, and what he could see of the walls, reminded him of his hotel room. Why was he here? Where had he been?

Images of a street and buildings and a long black limo flooded his mind.

"Dotty." The word came out as a barely audible croak, although he'd meant to shout it.

"Are you awake, Boss?" The voice belonged to Jones.

Mostyn tried to get up.

"Whoa, Boss." Jones put his hand on Mostyn's chest and gently pushed him back down. "Hang on a minute."

Jones got out his phone, made a call, and after a moment said, "He's awake." Call ended, Jones returned the phone to his pocket.

"Where's Dotty?"

"We were kinda hoping you'd tell us."

Mostyn got up on his elbows. "What do you mean?"

The door opened and in walked a man, followed by Dr. Bardon.

"Ah, Pierce, my boy, good to see you awake."

"Thank you, sir," Mostyn replied.

Bardon introduced the man with him. "This is Dr. Addison Clarke. He's been monitoring you since you were unceremoniously dumped on the hotel steps. Thanks to Mr. Jones, we were able to get to you before the paramedics arrived. Wouldn't do to have you in a civilian hospital."

"Dumped?" Confusion was written all over Mostyn's face. He shook his head. "Where's Dotty?"

"We were hoping you could tell us," Bardon said. "Her subdermal tracker is being blocked."

"I don't know where she is." Mostyn then explained about the attempt to run him over, the javelin attack, and finally the abduction. "I don't recall anything after the powder, until now."

"Very interesting," Bardon replied. "It appears this Asian fellow knows a thing or two about spells. It also seems he has our Dr. Kemper."

"We have to find Dotty," Mostyn said.

"We will," Bardon replied. "But first let Dr. Clarke have a look at you."

Bardon stepped back and the doctor moved next to the bed to begin his examination. After listening with his stethoscope, shining a light in Mostyn's eyes and throat, and testing his reflexes, Addison Clarke seemed satisfied Mostyn was okay.

"Good," Bardon said. "Thank you, Doctor. I'll take it from here."

Clarke wished everyone a good day, and left.

"The team is in Conference Room C," Bardon said. "Get dressed, and we'll join them. Come with me, Mr. Jones."

Bardon and Jones retired to the outer sitting room, closing the door behind them.

Mostyn got out of bed, took a quick shower, after which he began dressing. He was knotting his tie when his phone rang. He picked it up.

"Good afternoon, Mr. Mostyn." The ancient and ethereal sounding British voice.

"Where's—"

"She's well. And she will continue to be well if you leave by tonight. Once you have left Los Angeles, she will be released."

"How do I—"

"You want proof. I expected as much. Jot down the link and password I am about to give you. Both will be good for the next fifteen minutes. Are you ready?"

"Go ahead."

The voice gave Mostyn the information, which he jotted down.

"Safe travels, Mr. Mostyn." The voice was gone and there was only silence in its place.

Mostyn brought up the website on his phone and typed in the password. The site opened revealing a blank video screen. He tapped the "Join Conversation" button, and Dotty appeared on the computer screen.

"Dotty! Can you hear me?"

"I can hear you, Pierce. Enable your video so I can see you. Can you see me?"

"I can." He enabled the video so she could see him.

"How do you like the outfit? Should I get one for home?" Dotty was dressed in a one piece, long yellow silk dress with a white flower print. It had a high collar and sleeves extending a couple inches passed her elbow. There was a long side split on both sides which showed Dotty's legs up to a little bit above the middle of her thighs.

"Looks nice. Sure, get one for home. Are you okay?"

"I'm fine. But I won't be if you don't leave."

"What do you mean?"

"I was told the eldest grandson has, and I quote, 'taken a fancy to me'. If you don't leave, I will become his mistress. Or maybe even his wife."

Mostyn clenched his fists.

Dotty continued. "I was also told the grandson isn't normal. I don't know what they mean by that, but I have a feeling it's not something I want to find out."

"Don't worry, Dot. My uncle will fix things."

"Pierce, I'm scared, and you know I don't say that very often."

"Don't worry, Dot. Hang in there."

"I love you, Pierce."

Before Mostyn could answer her, the masked man appeared. In that ancient and ethereal tone of voice he said, "Y'ah hafh'drm gof'nn mgahnnn shuggnglui llll 'drn ah nog." Then the screen went blank.

Mostyn finished tying his tie, and joined Bardon and Jones. "I just talked to Dotty."

"How?" Jones asked.

"The wonders of modern technology, Jones. The masked man phoned me and gave me a link to a website so I could talk with her. It seems if I don't leave, Dotty becomes the wife or plaything for the weird grandson of the masked man. She's scared, Dr. Bardon. And you know Dotty doesn't scare easily."

"Did the masked man say anything?" Bardon asked.

"He did. I think it was R'lyehian."

"Oh, dear, my boy. Can you repeat it?"

"I think so." And Mostyn repeated the message to the best of his ability.

Bardon listened, pondered it for a minute or two, then said, "If you've repeated it correctly, the masked man said, 'I am the Summoner of the Spawn preparing the gate, or way, for the One Who is coming."

9

WHEN MOSTYN, Bardon, and Jones entered the conference room, they found everyone in a tizzy. It took Mostyn only a moment to determine why. On the wall opposite the windows, in bright red, were the words the man with the mask had said to him.

Winifred Petrie, on seeing Bardon, pointed at the wall and asked, "What does it say?"

Bardon replied with a question, "When did the words appear?"

"About ten minutes ago," Otto Stoppen answered.

"That's about the time you were talking to Dr. Kemper, my boy. Wasn't it?" Bardon said to Mostyn.

"Yes, sir, it was."

"He has a flair for showmanship," Bardon said.

"Who does, sir?" NicAskill asked.

"Our adversary," Bardon replied. To everyone, he said, "Please take your seats. We need to make an important decision."

Everyone sat and the room became quiet.

Bardon pointed to the writing on the wall. "We are not dealing with an ordinary thug. The words mean—," and Bardon told the team his rough translation of the message on the wall. "He calls himself a *summoner*, which means he is a follower, a fanatical follower, of the Great Old Ones. He is dangerous to the extreme. We don't know what he knows, but he knows enough to suspect Special Agent Mostyn is someone who might thwart him."

"What about Dr. Kemper?" Harbin Hammerschmidt asked.

"Our nameless adversary has her prisoner. The price for her freedom is Special Agent Mostyn's departure."

NicAskill raised her hand, and said, "Dr. Bardon," and he indicated she should continue. She asked, "How do we know he'll let Dr. Kemper go?"

The director shrugged. "We don't. So the question before us is, do we give him what he wants in the hope he releases Dr. Kemper? Or do we ignore him?"

"If we ignore him," Mostyn began, "Dotty said she'd be given to his grandson as a mistress or wife — and she added the grandson is apparently not normal."

"What does that mean?" Jones asked.

"She didn't know," Mostyn answered.

"If this guy is a fan of the Great Old Ones," Baker said, "then his grandson not being normal might not actually be something we want to contemplate."

"Indeed, Mr. Baker," Bardon said.

"If we assume the masked man doesn't know about us, then maybe we can deceive him," Mostyn volunteered.

Bardon smiled. "Yes, we could. Do you have anything specific in mind?"

"A tulpa."

"Ah, yes, that might work quite nicely," Bardon said. He thought a moment before continuing. "You won't be able to make one, because we don't have months at our disposal for you to learn how to do so. I will have to create one that looks like you."

"You mind my asking what is this tulpa thing?" Jones said.

"Not at all, Special Agent Jones," Bardon said. "Tulpa creation is a Tibetan Buddhist practice. Normally the tulpa begins life in your mind. It more or less becomes a sentient being."

"You mean like another person in my head?" Jones asked.

"Yes," Bardon replied. "If the person creating the tulpa has sufficient power, the tulpa can actually take shape and be seen by others, as well as interact with them. The tulpa can also be sent on missions."

"So you're going to create this tulpa thing to look like Mostyn and send it home on a plane," Petrie said.

"That's the idea," Mostyn replied.

"Will it work?" Petrie asked.

Bardon smiled. "Yes, I think it will work. Time, however, is of the essence. We need to get started right away."

"Then let's do it," Mostyn said.

"And we'll also find out if this guy is honorable and will release Dr. Kemper," Baker added.

———

Mostyn, Jones, and Stoppen were in the room with Bardon. Kymbra NicAskill stood outside, guarding the room; making sure there were no intruders. The remaining team members were in the conference room watching what was going on via their computers.

To Mostyn, seeing Dr. Rafe Bardon in his three-piece suit sitting in the Lotus Position, was comical. Except what they were trying to do wasn't comical at all, but a matter of life or death. Dotty Kemper's life or death, for starters.

For an hour, Mostyn watched Bardon sit there on the bed with his eyes closed and his lips barely moving. He had no idea if Bardon had been successful or not.

However not much more time passed when a filmy white shape began forming on the bed next to him. The thing looked as tangible as a stream of smoke from a burning cigarette. Mostyn smiled. Bardon had created a tulpa. Now the question was, could he make the thing solid in time to catch the last flight out of Los Angeles.

The minutes passed into hours. The filmy ghost-like shape didn't move, nor did it gain any substantial substance. Mostyn looked at the clock. They had but three and a half hours to go before midnight. He glanced at the tulpa and then took a second look. The thing was no longer a smoke-like wraith. It now looked human. In fact, the thing looked a lot like him. The creature was still transparent, but it did have shape and form and looked like his twin.

More minutes slipped by. While Mostyn watched, the tulpa gradually became denser.

"It looks just like you, Mostyn," Stoppen said.

Mostyn chuckled. "The twin I never had."

"I think Dr. Bardon is almost finished," Stoppen said. "I can't see through it anymore."

"You're right," Mostyn agreed.

The tulpa opened its eyes. "Hello Special Agent in Charge Pierce Mostyn, and hello to you, Dr. Otto Stoppen."

"It sounds just like you, Mostyn," Stoppen exclaimed.

A look of disapproval crossed the creature's face. "I am not an *it*. I am a *he*."

Mostyn laughed. "He even wants to choose his own pronouns."

Bardon's eyes opened. "For all practical purposes, he is you, Pierce, my boy. He is developing his own personality, and will continue to do so."

"I am ready for this mission," the tulpa said.

"Very good, Special Agent Mostyn," Bardon said. "Let us be on our way."

10

MOSTYN AND BARDON, both in heavy disguise, watched the tulpa board the plane with no problems. Mostyn scanned the airport crowd looking for some sign of the masked man's henchmen, but saw nothing unusual in the people waiting to get on the plane or in those who were sitting nearby.

"If they're here," he whispered to Bardon, "they must be in disguise, too."

"They may not even be visible," Bardon whispered back. "It's also possible no one is here and the Summoner is watching remotely."

Mostyn nodded. He looked at his watch. Half-past eleven. They'd met the deadline. Once the door to the jet was closed that was it, the tulpa was on his way to New York and Dotty should be released. He clenched his fists. And then he was going after the bastard.

The door to the jetway closed. "Well, Pierce, my boy, let's head back. We have a lot to talk about."

Mostyn and Bardon exited the airport and walked out to the parking ramp, where Jones was waiting with the sedan. Once in the car, Bardon began talking.

"Let me bring you up to date, Pierce, my boy. You were drugged when the reports were sent out, and with everything happening..." He lifted his hands. "It will be simpler if I brief you."

"I can read the details later, sir."

"Indeed. We ran Mr. Cortado and Mr. Salzman through our database and all those we have access to. Thanks to Special Agent NicAskill's photographs, we were also able to run their faces through the databases as well. We got hits all around. Mr. Salzman is an experienced con artist. His known aliases are Milton Gray, Gary Salzman, Gray M Salzman, and Shlomo Salzman."

"What's his racket?"

"Just about everything, but art fraud seems to be his specialty."

Mostyn nodded. "Explains why he's hooked up with Cortado."

"It does, at least in part. Mr. Cortado is also something of a con artist, although nowhere near as successful as Mr. Salzman. Mr. Cortado is suspected of forging the works of Pilar Hernandez-Vega, Joan Miró, and Leonora Varo."

"Why only suspected?"

"Because the possible victims, thus far, are not willing to come forward and admit they were conned."

"I see."

"He also tried to impersonate the Hungarian artist

Lorine Kiss, at a time when Mr. Kiss was unable to leave Hungary."

"I take it he got caught."

"He did. Mr. Cortado had the misfortune of an acquaintance of Kiss's visit the show, and the woman blew the whistle on him, as you Americans say."

Mostyn chuckled. "What happened?"

"The scam of course was discovered. The paintings were confiscated and Mr. Cortado got five years probation. That's when he left New York for California."

"He could do that?"

Bardon shrugged. "He got someone here in California to offer him a job as an art restorer. Bogus, I'm sure. But it worked, and here he is."

"Very interesting. So what's with the statues?"

Bardon rubbed his hands together. "Ah, the statues. As near as our science staff can determine they are genuinely made of stone. A type of marble. And they were probably once living beings. At least that is what the sculptors said who examined the statues. They couldn't be carved. In addition, we lifted fingerprints from the woman."

"Seriously?"

"Yes, That's how fine the detail is."

"Amazing."

"It is."

"Could you identify her?"

"Yes, because we are able to access the California DMV records and the fingerprints they require for licenses."

"Is that legal, sir?"

"Need to know, my boy, need to know."

"I'll take that as a *no*."

Bardon merely smiled, and went on. "Her name was Fiorella Josephina Flores-Hernández. She lost her job about a year ago, her apartment four months later, and has apparently been homeless the past three or four months."

"And now she's dead."

"Sadly, yes. I asked Special Agent NicAskill and Dr. Petrie to talk to her family. Hopefully they'll have something for us tomorrow."

"Anything further on the book?"

"We found the high end bookseller in New York. He told us he got the book from a dealer in Munich, who bought it from a rare book collector's estate. Apparently the children were selling off everything to get cash."

Mostyn laughed. "The Munich dealer probably got a good price. I can't believe the heirs weren't aware of what they had on their hands."

"I quite agree, my boy. A costly mistake on their part."

"So how did the book get out here?"

"The New York dealer has a select clientele for certain esoteric items, and one of those clients lived out here. A Beverly Fitzroy McCandless."

"Where does she live?"

"Not a *she*, my boy."

"A *man* with the name Beverly?"

"Yes," Bardon replied, with a smile on his face. "Long before the fairer sex appropriated the name, Beverly was a male name. Quite British, you know."

"Huh. Learn something new every day. So where does *he* live?"

"He lives nowhere. He was murdered some three months after he bought the book and the book is missing. Apparently stolen."

"So we still don't know who has it."

"No, we don't. Although Mr. McCandless kept a diary and in the diary recorded getting several phone calls from someone who wanted the book and was willing to offer him a lot of money for it."

"And his turning down the offer resulted in his death."

"So it seems, my boy, so it seems."

"Did you get my people's reports?"

"Ah, yes, their nosing around the art community. The general consensus is that Mr. Cortado arrived in Los Angeles about five years ago. He is considered to be generally good, but not inspired, and did not start being a name until Mr. Salzman became his agent. Which just so happens to coincide with our learning about the book."

"So nothing new, there."

"Afraid not."

"Did NicAskill learn anything from Pitkin?"

"The only new piece of information is that Mr. Cortado did not create sculpture before meeting Mr. Salzman."

"Interesting. He sure got proficient fast."

Bardon chuckled. "Indeed he did, my boy. Indeed he did."

Jones pulled the limo into the hotel garage and stopped by a door. Bardon and Mostyn got out of the vehicle, maintaining their disguises, and walked to a room registered to one Diamond Jim Brady. Once inside, Bardon texted a message on his phone. Two people looking like hotel cleaning staff, moved down the hall. The equipment in the cleaning cart swept the corridor for bugs and spy cameras. When they found none, they texted an all clear back to Bardon.

"Good. We can get out of these disguises," Bardon said.

"If it's okay with you, sir, I'll keep mine on. Just in case."

Bardon nodded, and removed his. When he was back to looking like himself, he and Mostyn walked to the conference room. Jones had gotten there before them.

"The tulpa boarded the plane," Bardon told the team. "Now we wait."

"So we have no idea when or where our masked man will release Dr. Kemper?" Baker said.

"Unfortunately, no, Mr. Baker, we do not," Bardon answered.

The OUP director's phone chimed. He took it out of his pocket and looked at the screen. Bardon turned to Mostyn. "Check your phone, Mr. Mostyn. Our tulpa received a text on his phone which we cloned from yours, so you should have it as well."

Mostyn looked at his phone and read the text. A cloud descended on his face.

"What is it, Boss?" Jones asked.

"The bastard has decided to keep Dotty. It seems he has a further use for her."

11

MOSTYN DIDN'T SLEEP WELL in spite of Dr. Bardon's help. All night he dreamed of Dotty, and the dreams weren't good. Finally, at a quarter past six he got up, showered, and dressed, and went to the conference room. He was surprised to see Dr. Bardon there, drinking tea and smoking his pipe.

"Ah, Pierce, my boy, sit down. May I pour you a cup of tea, or do you wish to wait for coffee?"

"I'll wait for the coffee." Mostyn took a seat.

"They should be bringing it soon."

"What are you doing here, sir, if I may ask?"

"Thinking. I'll be leaving later this morning."

Mostyn nodded. He knew better than to ask the boss what he was thinking about. If Bardon wanted him to know he'd tell him, and Bardon said nothing. Mostyn got up and went to the window. He looked out over the Los Angeles skyline. Out there somewhere was Dotty Kemper, the ancient book they were after, and the masked man.

"I know what Dotty means to you, Pierce. However, the book is the top priority."

Mostyn turned and faced his boss. "Do you, sir?" Mostyn kept his voice steady.

"Yes, Pierce, I do. And I care about her, as well. Not in the same manner as you, but I do care. I am human, Pierce. Sometimes, all too human. I understand your feelings. I have lived and loved too."

Mostyn took a deep breath and exhaled. "The mission first. Yes, sir, I understand." Mostyn turned back to look out the window.

In a moment, Bardon was standing next to him. "This job we do is very difficult. Very difficult. There are days when I would like nothing better than to walk away and spend the remainder of my time on this lovely planet reading novels, drinking port and tea, and smoking my pipe."

"Truly, sir?"

"Yes, Pierce, truly." Bardon put his hand on Mostyn's shoulder. "We have, however, a higher calling."

"Yes, sir."

The door opened and in came Jones, NicAskill, and Dr. Stoppen, followed by the hotel staff person with the breakfast cart.

"Good morning, Los Angeles!" Jones said. "And to you, Dr. Bardon, and to you, Boss."

Mostyn and Bardon turned around, and at the same time said, "Jones." They extended morning greetings to the others and took their seats at the table. When the cart was empty and the staff person was wheeling it away, the remaining team members arrived.

Bardon stood and indicated everyone still standing should take a seat. "I'll be leaving shortly. Your mission is, firstly, to find the book and, secondly, to retrieve Dr. Kemper. I've briefed Special Agent in Charge Mostyn on the things he missed while drugged. I have confidence you'll succeed, and look forward to your return. I leave the briefing in Special Agent Mostyn's very capable hands." The director wished everyone a good day and left.

Mostyn stood and while walking to the head of the table couldn't help but think that the director's eyes had lingered a moment on Dr. Stoppen as he wished everyone a good day. Then again, given his present mood, he could have just been imagining it.

"As Dr. Bardon said, he briefed me on what's been happening. Did he say anything to you, while I was out of action?"

"Nope," Jones said. "Told us you'd fill us in."

"Very well." Mostyn went on and told his team what Bardon had told him the night before. When he finished, he entertained questions.

NicAskill was first. "Cortado didn't carve those statues. That I think is obvious. Even without the opinion of the geeks in the lab. So the question is, how did those people get turned to stone? Does this have something to do with the book we're looking for?"

"The answer to your second question, Agent NicAskill," Dr. Stoppen said, "is very likely. Dr. Bardon believes there is a ritual in the book which will summon or create a Gorgon."

"What's that?" Jones asked.

"The Medusa?" Stoppen said.

"You mean that woman who was so butt ugly she turned people to stone?" Jones asked.

Stoppen, a smile on his face, said, "That's one way of putting it."

"So what you're telling us," NicAskill said, "is that we're dealing with a mythological creature here."

Stoppen nodded. "That's what Dr. Bardon believes. Only it isn't a myth."

"Let me get this straight," Jones said. "There's a butt ugly woman running around LA turning people to stone. Like those statues we found in the art gallery."

"That's what he's saying," Hammerschmidt said.

"Yes," Stoppen confirmed. "Whoever has the book, has created or unleashed a Gorgon."

NicAskill sat back in her chair and muttered, "Well I'll be damned."

"Why the hell didn't he tell us this to begin with?" Dr. Petrie asked.

"Correct me if I'm wrong, Dr. Stoppen," Mostyn said. "It's because Bardon wasn't sure. Our discovery of the statues confirmed his suspicion."

Stoppen nodded.

"Any other questions?" Mostyn asked. When no one replied, he continued, "Okay, let's move on. NicAskill and Dr. Petrie, you spoke with the family of Fiorella Flores-Hernández?"

"We did," NicAskill said.

"And it's a good thing we know Spanish," Petrie added.

"What did you find out?" Mostyn asked.

"Fiorella lost her job thirteen months ago," NicAskill began. "She was a secretary at FAZ Logistics. She was unable to find another job and her roommate kicked her out when she didn't pay the rent. She lived with her parents in Avocado Heights, but she wore out her welcome and started staying with extended family and friends until she pretty much wasn't welcomed anywhere. At that point she ended up staying in the parks downtown."

"And disappeared," Petrie said. "Her family lost contact with her."

"Until she showed up at an art exhibit as a statue," NicAskill added, and after a pause said, "Her mother gave us a picture so we could find her. They, her mother and father, feel terribly guilty. They feel they should have had more patience with her."

Mostyn looked out the window. *Like so many homeless*, he thought, *she ends up in the big city. The cold, cruel, heartless city. Dotty's somewhere in this city.*

His eyes took in the buildings and the streets. In the distance he saw two jets. His mind drifted to the masked man. The Chinese-looking mask. The Chinese robe he wore. The voice.

He turned back to his team sitting around the table, watching him. "He's Chinese. The masked man is Chinese. Maybe originally from Hong Kong. Dr. Stoppen, I'd like you and Willie Lee to visit every antique bookstore in LA."

"We can do that. I know who all the important dealers are."

"Good. Find out every scrap of gossip about the book that you can. Report back here by seven tonight. The rest of us are going to Chinatown."

———

Mostyn sent Jones and Hammerschmidt to the north end of Chinatown with instructions to work their way south. NicAskill and Petrie were to begin at the opposite end and move north, the two teams meeting somewhere in the middle.

As for himself, he had a different task. He went to the county recorder's office and began looking through the platt books to get an idea as to who owned what in Los Angeles. The clerk gave him no trouble whatsoever, even showed him to a desk he could use. Such was the power of his IRS ID badge.

Taking no chances, Mostyn had put on his disguise. A dark brown wig to cover his strawberry blond crewcut. A fake mustache and Van Dyke beard in the same color as the wig. He'd used a makeup pencil to color in his eyebrows, and he wore a pair of glasses with dark brown frames.

He carefully examined the books, often resorting to a magnifying glass, paying particular attention to Chinatown. It took him a couple of hours of looking at a myriad of names to notice a pattern of holdings by the Ching Wo Company, Inc. He took pictures of the platt book and texted the address of the Ching Wo Company back to head-quarters requesting information.

With the request sent off, Mostyn flagged down one of the clerks. "Say, can you tell me if there's any significance as to why someone would want properties along this route, and this one?"

The man followed the two routes Mostyn pointed out. After a minute or so, he said, "Beats me. The old subway ran along this route." He pointed to the map. "Don't know if there's any significance."

"What about this one?"

The man shrugged. "Those properties are on top of some of the old tunnels under LA."

"What were the tunnels used for?"

"Beats me. I think they were service tunnels. Gangsters used them during Prohibition, so I've heard, to transport booze. There were even bars down there. The King Eddy used to be down there. A music store was the cover. Now the bar is where the music store was. You can still access the tunnels from there."

"Thank you."

"Sure. Don't mention it."

Mostyn smiled. Everything was beginning to come together.

12

WHILE MOSTYN WAS EXAMINING platt books and learning about the old LA subway and the other tunnels beneath Los Angeles, Jones and Dr. Hammerschmidt drove to the north end of Chinatown. Their first stop was the Chinese Catholic Church.

"Why are we stopping here?" Hammerschmidt asked.

"Because it's this way, Harbin, priests and ministers know a lot about the community. They circulate, visit people, people tell them things they wouldn't dream of telling anyone else. I'll be very surprised if we don't get something of value from Father Paul Chang."

Jones and the chemist walked into the church. The lighting was dim, and the cool air felt good, for the day was promising to be a hot one. The men scanned the interior looking for a sign indicating where they would find the office.

"Why don't we try that door," Hammerschmidt said, pointing to a door off to the side of the altar.

"Sure, why not?"

The men walked over to the door, and Jones opened it. There was a smallish room with a door leading outside, and two other doors, one of which was marked "Office".

Jones walked over to the door marked "Office", and opened it.

A young Chinese woman looked up, smiled, and asked how she might help them.

"We'd like to talk to Father Chang," Jones said.

"I'm sorry. He's at prayers right now."

Jones held up his ID for her to see. "I don't mean to be disrespectful, but it's important that we see him now."

The young woman looked from the ID to Jones, her face clouded with fear.

"You don't have to worry," Jones assured her. "We are not here because the church did anything wrong."

She breathed a sigh of relief, and stood. "I'll tell him you're here. Please have a seat." She left, and the OUP agents, masquerading as agents of the IRS, sat in the hard plastic chairs.

After a few minutes she returned and told them the priest would see them in his office, which was the room next door. Jones thanked her, and he and Hammerschmidt left.

Jones knocked on the door of the priest's office, and when a voice said, "Come in", he opened the door and walked in, with Hammerschmidt following.

"I'm Father Chang. How may I help you?"

Jones answered, "We're looking for a rare book. Has anyone in your parish seen or heard about a rare book?"

"What kind of book?" the priest asked.

"The kind your church would have burned back in the Middle Ages," Jones replied.

"Some kind of book on sorcery?"

"You could say that," Jones said.

The priest thought a moment before speaking, and when he did start speaking he glanced at the crucifix hanging on the wall.

"I hear lots of stories. Most of them are routine and mundane. Some, though, are quite unusual. Those said in the confessional are said with the understanding that they are confidential."

Jones said, "I understand."

"Several weeks ago, an old man told me his grandson was involved with a great lord, the grandson had bragged that things were going to start changing soon because the great lord had a book that gave him tremendous power, and that he, the grandson, was going to be an important man."

"Did the grandson say where the book was?" Hammerschmidt asked.

The priest shook his head, and looked at Hammerschmidt. "No. Just that it was in a safe location deep underground."

"Did the old man say anything else about this book?" Jones asked.

"No. He was more concerned about how to protect his grandson from the evil forces he thought were at work."

"What kind of evil forces?" Jones asked.

"Demonic powers."

Jones nodded, while Hammerschmidt asked the priest if he believed in demons.

"I do," Chang replied. "There is good and there is evil in the world. God the Father and our Lord Jesus Christ," the priest crossed himself, "will have the ultimate victory. In the meantime, I believe the words of scripture: the devil goes about as a roaring lion, seeking whom he may devour."

"Do you have any idea who this great lord might be?" Jones asked.

"There is a legend," Chang began, "that a young Chinese man came to America in the eighteen seventies. This young man's name was Wing Lee and he had been a powerful wizard in China. His downfall came about because he was arrogant. He challenged an older wizard to a duel and lost. Wing Lee fled China and came to America under the Burlingame Treaty. He worked as a coolie building the levees here in California.

"Around eighteen eighty, he was working as a scab and got involved in a race riot, where it is said his face was disfigured. He took to wearing a mask to hide the disfigurement and eventually he came to Los Angeles and set up a tea and herb store with the money he'd saved. His business began to thrive and he married."

"Sounds like a typical immigrant story," Jones said.

Father Chang nodded. "Yes, it does. However, Wing Lee's wife was very young. After she bore him four sons and two daughters, she left him for a rich white man. Wing Lee was devastated and vowed revenge. It is said, he returned to sorcery and through magic eventually gained control of Chinatown and a large portion of the valley."

"And what does this story have to do with the great lord?" Hammerschmidt asked.

"It is rumored that Wing Lee still lives and that he is the great lord."

"That should be easy enough to disprove," Jones said. "After all he should be dead by now."

The priest nodded. "Should be. But Wing Lee disappeared shortly before World War One. There is no death certificate. Many Chinese believe he is still alive. They say he has prolonged his life by means of blasphemous rituals. And that he will eventually destroy the white man for stealing his wife."

Jones raised his eyebrows.

Hammerschmidt asked, "Are there any photographs of Wing Lee?"

"Not to my knowledge," Chang replied.

"Is the family still here?" Jones asked.

"They are," Chang said, "but they are very secretive. No one has knowingly seen them in decades."

"So who is the old man's grandson involved with?" Jones asked.

Father Chang shrugged. "I don't know, and as far as I can tell the old man doesn't know either."

Jones stood and Hammerschmidt followed. "Thank you for your time, Father."

"Sorry I couldn't be of more help."

"Oh, I wouldn't say that," Jones replied. "You've been very helpful."

Jones and Hammerschmidt walked outside.

"Where did the sun go?" Jones asked, for the sky was covered with dark gray and black clouds.

Hammerschmidt pointed. "Look at that vortex. Looks like a tornado is forming."

"It sure as hell does," Jones said. "Come on, let's get to the car." He took out his phone to make sure the conversation had been recorded, and seeing that it had, he slipped the phone back into his pocket, and ran over to the car. He unlocked it and got in, the chemist right behind him.

The two watched the wind pick up debris from the streets and carry it up into the air.

"That vortex is heading right for the church," Hammerschmidt said.

"Kind of weird, isn't it?"

"I think so."

When the vortex was over the church, the two OUP operatives watched a swirling cone descend and saw the rotating black funnel rip up roof tiles, as though it was a giant drill tearing a hole into the building. And then, after a moment or two, the funnel withdrew.

Jones and Hammerschmidt watched the black and gray clouds disappear as quickly as they had arrived, and in their place a thin sheet of cirrostratus clouds drifted lazily in a brilliant blue sky.

"What the hell did we just see?" Hammerschmidt said.

"I don't know, but we'd better check out the church."

The two men got out of the car, ran over to the church, and entered the building. There was no damage to the sanctuary. They walked back to the office area. There they saw a circular hole in the roof and nothing but debris and litter where the two offices had been.

13

WHILE JONES and Hammerschmidt were at the Chinese Catholic Church. NicAskill and Dr. Petrie were talking to shop owners on the south end of Chinatown.

"These people seem awfully tight-lipped, don't you think?" Petrie said.

"They do at that," NicAskill agreed. "I think they're scared, and scared people aren't going to talk unless they know there won't be any repercussions from talking."

"We're telling them we're the IRS. Can't get much bigger or more powerful than that."

"Perhaps, Dr. Petrie, but we don't live here. Once we're gone, we're gone. The people they're afraid of will still be here."

"I suppose you're right."

"Let's change tactics." NicAskill opened the shop door. "Just follow my lead," she whispered and walked in; Petrie behind her.

NicAskill walked up to the counter. The only other

people in the shop looked to be tourists. Behind the counter was an old woman. NicAskill said, "Hi! Are you the owner?"

The old woman looked at NicAskill, her face blank, then turned and yelled a stream of words in a language that wasn't English. In a moment, a young attractive woman pushed aside a bead curtain and stepped behind the counter.

"Hi! How may I help you?"

"We're with Around the World Realty and we're looking for the owner."

"The owner?"

NicAskill smiled and nodded.

The young woman turned to the older woman and started speaking in whatever language it was they spoke. The old woman answered, and the young woman turned back to NicAskill.

"I'm sorry, but my grandmother doesn't know who owns the building. All of the shop keepers have a lease with Golden Dragon Management Company. They handle everything."

"Thank you," NicAskill said. "Do you happen to have an address or phone number?"

The young woman turned to the old woman and said something. The old woman replied. The young woman turned back to NicAskill. "Excuse me. My grandmother thinks there's a business card in the office. One moment, please."

"Sure. Thank you," NicAskill said.

The young woman disappeared behind the beaded

curtain. NicAskill turned away and began looking at a tea set. Petrie picked up a vase and looked at the price tag on the bottom.

"What? They want two hundred and fifty for *this*? Outrageous."

NicAskill cast a glance Petrie's way. "It's pretty."

"Not for two-fifty it isn't."

The young woman returned, and NicAskill stepped back up to the counter. The young woman slid a sheet of paper over to NicAskill. "I made a copy of the card for you."

NicAskill picked up the paper, thanked her, and headed for the door. Petrie was already out on the sidewalk.

When NicAskill was standing next to her, Petrie asked, "Does it look legit?"

I don't know," NicAskill replied. "There's one way to find out." She took out her phone and dialed the number. After a moment, she put the phone away.

"Went straight to voicemail. We can set up a dummy return number and try again."

"What about email?"

NicAskill looked at the copy of the card. "They have an email address. We'll have to set up a dummy email account."

"Now what?" Petrie asked.

"We keep doing what we've been doing. Let's try the real estate ploy at that restaurant over there."

NicAskill and Petrie crossed the street and entered the restaurant. A young woman smiled at them and asked if there were just the two of them.

"We'd like to speak to the owner, if possible," NicAskill said.

The smile disappeared and a look of concern took over her face. "I hope there is no problem. The owner is not here. I am his daughter. Perhaps I can help?"

NicAskill said, "We're with Around the World Realty and we're prepared to make a good offer to buy the building."

Relief replace concern and her smile returned.

"The building? My father does not own the building. We lease this space."

"I see," NicAskill said. "Do you know who does own the building?"

"No, I'm afraid not. We pay the Golden Dragon Management Company. That's who our lease is with."

NicAskill took out the photocopy and showed it to the woman. "Is this the company?"

"I think so. My dad is the one who mainly does the books and pays the bills. I help him sometimes. The address looks familiar."

"Thank you. You've been most helpful." NicAskill turned and left. Petrie followed.

Out on the sidewalk, Petrie said, "I bet Golden Dragon manages everything here."

"Maybe not the banks, or the hospital," NicAskill replied. "But for these small shops?" She shook her head. "I won't wager against you."

"Let's try a few more," Petrie said, "might as well see if there's any competition."

The two walked to a small store selling traditional

Chinese medicine. The owner leased the space from Golden Dragon. The smoke shop next door leased their space from Golden Dragon as well. The next block, Golden Dragon was replaced by Black Lotus Management Company.

"Both companies have headquarters here in Los Angeles," NicAskill observed. She took out her phone and did a search. "Rather odd, Winifred, there's no website for either company. No reviews either."

"That is odd. Especially in this day and age."

"They're not on social media, either. At least not the main platforms."

"Very odd."

"It's as if they don't want to advertise their presence."

"Maybe they don't need to. If they only do business in Chinatown."

NicAskill looked skeptical. "Maybe. Still doesn't seem normal." She looked around. "Why don't we…"

"What?"

NicAskill pointed, and Petrie followed her finger. Roiling and churning gray and black clouds were rolling in from the east, blotting out the blue sky.

"What's going on?" Petrie said. "I didn't think we were supposed to get a storm."

"We aren't. Sunny and no rain."

"Doesn't look like it now."

"Sure doesn't."

They watched the clouds cover the sky and then begin to rotate.

"Oh, my God," Petrie said. "A tornado. I was in one once. It was the most terrifying thing in my life."

And then out of the swirling vortex a funnel of cloud dropped down. A moment later, the rotating cone withdrew, and the roiling clouds cleared leaving blue sky and filmy white clouds in their wake.

"What was that?" Petrie asked.

"I don't know. But Jones and Hammerschmidt are up there." NicAskill took out her phone and called Jones. "Jonesy, are you guys okay up there?"

Jones told her about his conversation with the priest and the destruction of the offices after they left the church.

"Something weird is going on here," NicAskill said. "Maybe we need to meet with the boss."

Jones concurred and said he'd call Mostyn.

NicAskill pocketed her phone. To Petrie, she said, "Some weird shit is going on. We're going back to the hotel to confer with the boss."

"What kind of weird shit?"

"That tornado?"

Petrie nodded.

"It punched a hole in the roof of the Chinese Catholic Church and destroyed two offices. No sign of the priest or the secretary. And the priest had just told Jones and Hammerschmidt a very interesting story about the guy who might be our masked man."

14

DR. DOTTY KEMPER'S temper was on a very short fuse. She had no complaints about the suite her captor had put her in. It was luxurious beyond anything she could dream of. The food they'd given her was exquisite. The bed was beyond comfortable and the silk sheets were decadence itself. There was a bookcase filled with books. The towels in the bathroom were the plushest and softest she'd ever felt. There were chairs and couches that were just like how she dreamed it would feel to sit on a cloud. Nor did she have a complaint about the beautiful silk cheongsam dresses hanging in the closet.

She looked around the spacious suite. It was magnificent, but she was a prisoner and that pissed her off.

She grabbed the breakfast tray and hurled it at the enormous window overlooking the city. Tray, plate, bowls, and leftover food hit the window and fell to the floor.

"Not even a goddamn scratch. Must be that transparent aluminum shit."

She picked up one of the dining table chairs and hurled it at the locked door. Yesterday, she'd destroyed three pillows, four vases, kicked one guard in the crotch, and decked a second one before she found herself staring at two pistols pointed towards her head. That calmed her for a while.

"I should've had Helene teach me how to dematerialize. Then I would've been out of here faster than they could say chop suey."

She threw herself on a chaise longue, and after a moment found herself rubbing her hand across the luxurious fabric.

"I've seen these in movies," she said out loud. "Never knew people actually used them. Might have to get myself one. That is, if I ever get out of here."

After a moment, she said, "And that's beginning to look like a no go."

She lay on her back, her knees up. "Houston, we have a problem. One lying sack of shit, who hides behind a mask."

There was a knock on the door and it opened. Two men stepped in. Young Chinese men in black suits, white shirts, and black ties. A third man came in behind them, older, but also wearing a black suit, white shirt, and black tie.

Dotty stood and moved behind the chaise longue.

Following the three men, came the masked man. He was wearing the traditional men's long gown in solid gold. The mask was also gold with a black beard and mustache painted on it. He walked with slow and deliberate steps. Behind him two young women carried a chair, which they set on the floor, and in which the masked man sat. Dotty looked daggers at him.

The masked man spoke. His softly sibilant voice sounded ancient and ethereal. "I hear, Dr. Kemper, that your accommodations do not please you."

"They're not mine."

"That is true. The accommodations are not yours." He paused, before continuing. "They could be yours, however."

"They're nice, but I prefer my own place. Thank you very much."

A chuckle came from the mask. "Unfortunately for you, Dr. Kemper, you will not be seeing your home again. However, I have a proposition for you. It is like those TV game shows. There are three doors. You pick a door and you get what is behind it. Unlike those shows, I will tell you what is behind each door."

"Very generous of you." Sarcasm dripped from Kemper's words.

Once again a chuckle came from the mask. "Actually it is. Your first option is to marry my grandson. You will produce children. Lots of children."

"I thought I was just supposed to be his plaything."

"Nothing is static, Dr. Kemper. I have a different plan now. So option number one for you is to marry my grandson."

"I don't think so."

"You haven't heard the other options."

Dotty gestured for him to continue.

"Option number two is that you will be the sacrifice

which will enable me to open the gate allowing the Nameless One access to this dimension."

Dotty shook her head. "Definitely not."

"Very well. Behind our door number three is what I call the zuvembie option."

"Which is?"

"Unlike the classic zuvembie, you won't be a mindless creature that only lives to kill. However, you will definitely no longer be in control of your mind. *I* will control your mind. You will be *my slave.*"

"I don't like that option either."

The Masked Man ignored her comment and continued. "You see, Dr. Kemper, it has come to my attention that people are looking for me. I do not fully understand who they are, or what resources they have available to them. What I do know is that they, and you, Dr. Kemper, for I know you are one of them, pose a threat to me. To the hegemony of my empire."

The masked man lifted his hands and shrugged. "Therefore, whoever you are, you all must be eliminated."

"Why don't you just pick my brain and then kill me?"

"I could. But then I would simply have information. I'd rather get full value from an asset such as yourself. So what is your decision, Dr. Kemper? Door number one? Door number two? Or door number three?"

"I have to decide right now? Don't I get some time to think this over?"

"Come now, Dr. Kemper. From your perspective there really is only one choice. It is the first option. You keep your mind and you get to live in luxury for the rest of your life. However, if you want some time to think things over, so be it. You have five minutes. Start thinking."

Dotty's eyes went from the masked man to the two women standing behind him, to the older man standing to one side, to the two men standing in front of where the masked man was sitting.

Five against one. Not very good odds. And then there was The Mask himself. He probably had a trick or two up his sleeves. She was not going to get out of this predicament alive. But she might die trying, and at this point that seemed to be her best option.

Door number four, she thought. *And may the Force be with me.*

Dotty walked around the chaise longue, placed the palms of her hands together, and bowed before The Mask. "I have made my decision."

"Good. Let's hear it."

Dotty stood up and launched herself at the young man on her right. She gave him a round house kick to the head that sent him sprawling. She pivoted just in time to deliver a kick to the solar plexus of the other young man that saw him drop to the floor like a rock.

The young women charged. Dotty's powerhouse punch sent the one woman flying.

Then there was a sharp pain and Dr. Dotty Kemper's world went black.

15

MOSTYN SAT AT THE TABLE. Plates of sandwiches, and carafes of coffee and water ran down the center of the table. The team members, except for Dotty Kemper, were eating and drinking. Mostyn, however, just sipped at a styrofoam cup of coffee. The coffee was just how he liked it: strong with a hefty dollop of cream, real cream.

He'd listened to the reports from Jones and Hammerschmidt, and NicAskill and Petrie. He'd told them what he'd discovered. Then the food arrived and he decided to let them eat before listening to what Stoppen and Baker had found out.

The coffee was hot. *Those are good carafes*, he thought. His mind drifted back to the morning before Bardon had sent Dotty and him out to attempt the capture of Tommy John MacIlhenney. Dotty had made coffee in her French Press. He liked her coffee. It was perfect. That was definitely one thing she did better than Helene. He smiled.

Helene and coffee were like an airplane defying gravity after it had run out of fuel.

Dotty. Would he ever see her again? And if he didn't, what would he do? He had Helene. But Dotty was Dotty. He'd worked with her for a long time and he'd loved her for a good portion of that time.

He looked at his styrofoam cup of coffee and thought of her making coffee, their coffee, that morning. It was perfect. It was always perfect. Now she was gone, and, in what might have been their last chat, he hadn't even told her he loved her.

They would get her back. They had to get her back. That was all there was to it.

He became aware of someone saying, "Boss!" He looked up. Jones. Jones was yelling, "Boss", and Baker was saying, "Earth to Mostyn. Come in Mostyn."

"I'm here. What is it?"

"Otto was telling us about his morning," Dr. Winifred Petrie said.

"Did you find out something of importance, Dr. Stoppen?" Mostyn asked.

"Yes and no," he replied.

"Okay. I'll take the good news first," Mostyn said.

"The buzz is that a very ancient book was purchased and brought to LA within the last year or so. The Huntington made an attempt to find who owned it, in order to make an offer to buy it. They were not successful. Two private collectors are also pursuing a purchase, but have yet to find the owner."

Mostyn nodded. "The bad news?"

"My contacts are of the opinion the book is just a legend at best, and a fake at worst."

Mostyn shook his head. "No. The book is real, otherwise Bardon wouldn't have us looking for it."

"So what do we do now, Boss?" NicAskill asked.

Mostyn took a deep breath, held it for a moment, and then exhaled. "I think we know four vital pieces of information. First, the book is real. I don't think there is any other way to explain the strange cloud formations. Second, the management companies and Ching Wo are fronts for whoever we are after. Third, the fact that the properties owned by Ching Wo are above an underground tunnel system seems to me to be intentional. And finally, all legends are based on truth. Consequently, we are either dealing with Wing Lee himself, or someone who has appropriated the legend. And in either case, the person commands great power. He is, for lack of a better word, a sorcerer of tremendous ability."

"That all makes sense, Boss, but what do we do with the information?" NicAskill asked.

"I think it's time we do a turn at urban spelunking, because my gut is telling me that's where we'll find the book."

"Aw, man," Jones blurted. "We're not going underground *again*? Tell me we're not."

"Were you listening, Jones?" Mostyn said.

With a smile on his face, Baker quipped, "You used the word 'spelunking'. That has a few too many syllables for Jones."

"Fork you, Mr. Camera Man," Jones said. "I know what

the word 'spelunking' means. I may have blonde hair, but I'm not dumb."

NicAskill punched him in the arm. "You just don't want to get cobwebs in those golden locks, right?"

"Shit," Jones muttered. "Fine. Back to being mole people. I love being a mole."

"You enjoyed K'n-yan," Mostyn said, with his best poker face.

Jones threw his hands up. "All right, all right. When do we take the tunnel tour?"

Mostyn's phone chimed. He took it out of his pocket and looked at it. When he was done reading, he put it back.

"The report on Ching Wo Company, Inc. came back. It's a shell company, owned by another shell company, that is also owned by a shell company, et cetera, et cetera. However, it seems the end of the line is a company in Taiwan. The Mo Yan Corporation. It is privately held, but no owners or officers have been found at this point."

"Is this relevant?" Dr. Stoppen asked.

"No," Mostyn replied. "I think it safe to say that Wing Lee, or his imposter, is the owner. And does the information alter anything for us? I don't think so. If anything, a Taiwanese company tends to re-enforce the legend."

"Do you believe we're actually dealing with this Wing Lee?" Petrie asked.

"Yes," Mostyn replied. "I've heard the voice. It was ancient sounding. Like a whisper emanating from a distant tomb."

"So where are we going to access the tunnel system?" NicAskill asked.

"There are two entrances that I'm aware of, and there are probably more. One is in the Hall of Records. An elevator, in fact, takes you there. The other is in a bar that was once a speakeasy located in the tunnels. The King Eddy. We'll try one of these first and go from there. Any further questions?"

No one said anything.

"Finish your lunch. We'll move out in forty-five minutes."

16

DOTTY OPENED HER EYES. The light was dim, barely holding at bay the Stygian blackness. She felt cold and realized she was lying on concrete. The surface was pitted and rough. She sat up and saw that she was chained to the concrete wall. An iron manacle was on each wrist. They were connected by a chain. Another chain ran from the concrete wall to the chain connecting the wrist manacles.

"Where the hell am I?" she said.

"You are in the tunnels below the city."

Dotty looked in the direction the voice came from and saw a man sitting in a chair on the edge of the darkness.

"Tunnels? Tunnels below LA?"

"Yes," he said. "They are old. Very old. Many sections are barricaded because they are in poor condition. Other sections are lost to memory because they were here long before the tunnels dug by men."

"Who are you?" Dotty asked.

"My name does not matter, Dr. Kemper. I am to watch you and make sure you are okay."

"Well, I'm not *okay*. I have a headache and I ache from lying on this concrete and I'm cold."

"I'm sorry. There is nothing I can do to alleviate your pain, or to provide you with warmth."

"Then what the hell good are you?"

"That question has no relevance. I simply serve the master. I am to watch you and make sure you are okay. That you are in no life threatening distress."

"I will be if you don't get me a blanket."

"I am sorry. I do not have a blanket for you."

"Fine. Be that way." Dotty stood. She turned around and pulled on the chain. *Seems solid enough,* she thought. *Too bad for me.*

She stretched the chain as far as it would go. *About four or five feet of play. At least I'm not up against the wall with my hands over my head.*

"Even if you were free of your shackles, you would not find your way to the surface."

"Thanks for the information," Dotty replied. She turned around to face the man on the edge of the darkness. "So I guess I'm not going to be the blushing bride, am I?"

"I do not know your fate. I only know that you gained the ire of the master."

"Well, that's just a goddamn shame, isn't it?"

"You do not want to anger the master."

"Between you and me? If I get my hands on that prick the only thing he'll be master of is worm food."

"You are in no position to make threats."

"Threats? Listen, you mechanical dildo, that was a promise. You need to learn the difference."

"You shouldn't make promises you cannot keep."

"Who appointed you to be my mother? Besides, how do you know I can't keep my promise?"

The man stood and stepped into the feeble light cast by the electric lantern. Dotty recognized him as the older man who'd come into her suite with the masked man.

"You are in grave danger, Dr. Kemper. You should not jest."

She snorted. "I don't believe in prayer, so that leaves me with jesting."

"That is too bad."

"What is too bad is that I didn't die up there in my room."

"That is true, Dr. Kemper. That is very true."

The elevator came to a stop and the door opened. Mostyn, NicAskill, Baker, and Petrie stepped out. The door closed and the elevator rose.

Mostyn took in the scene before him. They were underground and stretching away from them was a tunnel of large dimensions. The electric lighting was barely adequate and came from naked bulbs in rusted cages, spaced along the walls and ceiling.

The dingy concrete was decorated in multi-colored designs, words, slogans, and declarations of love. The floor was gritty and sticky in places. Plastic pop bottles, trash, discarded office equipment, and boxes of records littered the floor where it met the walls. Baker took a few photos.

After a couple of minutes the car returned with the rest of the team.

"Well, look at this," Jones said, pointing to the walls of the tunnel entrance, "Graffiti artists of the Underworld."

"Have wall, will paint," Baker quipped.

"For supposedly being off limits to the general public," NicAskill said, "this place seems to be pretty popular."

"Doesn't it?" Jones replied.

Baker, looking at a condom on the floor, said, "It never ceases to amaze me where people will decide to satisfy they're sexual urges."

Petrie made a sound of disgust.

NicAskill laughed. "Homo horny sapiens."

Mostyn clapped his hands. "Let's get ready, people."

The team members were wearing street clothes to minimize attention and not arouse suspicion. Each one had a backpack.

They opened their backpacks and took out their helmets, each was equipped with an attached electric lamp, a flashlight, and a weapon. The packs also contained water, emergency rations, spelunking equipment, and a lightweight space blanket.

Jones carried the special OUP issued phone which allowed the team to maintain contact with headquarters.

"Let Sumer Base know we are in the tunnels, will you, Jones?" Mostyn said.

"Sure thing, Boss." Jones made the call and when finished turned to Mostyn.

"They sent you a 3D map of the tunnels, Boss. We've also gotten a lucky break. Sumer Base has started receiving Dr. Kemper's subdermal transmitter signal again."

"That is good news," Mostyn said, while fishing his phone out of his pocket. When it was in hand, he tapped on it and displayed the 3D holographic map. A flashing green dot indicated where Dotty Kemper was located.

Mostyn studied the diagram for a moment and then called Jones and NicAskill over. "What do you make of this?" he asked.

The two special agents studied the hologram. Jones spoke first. "Doesn't that beat all. She's not even in one of the tunnels."

"More likely, she's in a tunnel that isn't on any map," NicAskill said.

"That's what I said," Jones replied.

"Yeah, right, Jones," NicAskill said. "And Einstein had marshmallows for brains."

Mostyn studied the holographic projection of the tunnel system. After several minutes, he declared, "We're going to rescue Dr. Kemper."

"We're supposed to look for the book," Dr. Stoppen said.

"And I'm willing to bet that where Dr. Kemper is, the book will be close by," Mostyn replied. "Now get your packs on, and follow me."

17

MOSTYN, phone in hand and the holographic map hovering above it, strode off down the tunnel, his team following. He keyed the mic on his helmet, which was tied into the transmitter-receiver on the special OUP phone Jones had.

"Sumer Base, this is Mostyn. Over."

"Didn't expect to hear from you, Mostyn. What can we do for you?"

"I'm reading your map and I see the dot marking Dr. Kemper's location. We're going to rescue her."

"That's not your primary objective."

"Maybe not, Langston, but my gut tells me that where Kemper is, the book is going to be somewhere nearby."

Mostyn heard the hesitation on the other end.

"Look, Langston, I'm not asking permission. We are going after Dr. Kemper. What I need from you is some direction. Where Kemper is on the hologram, there's no tunnel. I need you to provide some augmentation to the map you gave me."

"Okay, Mostyn, it's your call. You can deal with the director. I'll see what I can do. Keep me posted."

"My helmet cam is on. You'll see what I see."

"Sounds good. Let me do some further checking on the tunnel system. I'll get back to you."

"Roger, Langston, Mostyn out."

Mostyn and the others continued down the tunnel, the graffiti gradually petering out the further they traveled from the elevator. The nature of the debris on the floor also changed from what they'd initially seen to first lots of used condoms, food wrappers, and syringes, and then to broken pieces of concrete and brick, along with dangling conduits and broken pipe. He noticed a rodent in the opening of one of the broken pipes. It ran into the pipe as the team approached.

To his left was a barricaded tunnel entrance. Mostyn stopped in front of it.

"Where are we going, Boss?" Jones asked.

"To Chinatown. That seems to be where the action is."

"And we can get there from here?"

"We can, Jones, we can." He paused, looked at the rusting iron barrier, zoomed in on the map, and then said, "Okay, Jones, get to work and open this barrier."

Jones looked at the iron bars, which looked like misplaced wrought iron railings, and where they were bolted into the concrete walls on either side of the tunnel entrance. He turned to Mostyn, and said, "This isn't going to be easy."

"Then I suggest you quit dawdling and hop to it."

Jones shook his head, shrugged out of his backpack and set it on the floor. He opened the pack and began rummaging around inside. Out came what looked like a garrote, but it was in actuality a diamond encrusted wire saw. He set the saw on the floor by the barrier. The saw was followed by a cylinder. Jones unscrewed one end of the cylinder and took out a small cutting torch. He slipped on a pair of goggles. Mostyn picked up the saw and started working on the other side of the barrier. Jones ignited the torch and began cutting iron.

In about fifteen minutes the barrier was lying on the floor. Jones packed up the equipment and shrugged back into the backpack.

The team peered into the inky blackness of the tunnel. The beams from the seven electric lamps seemed feeble compared to the darkness. What they could see was damp and crumbling concrete and brick. Ten feet in was a sign hanging from the ceiling that warned them the tunnel had been deemed unsafe by the commissioner of public safety. The sign showed rust where the paint had chipped off.

"Sir," NicAskill said. "There's something I think you should see. I found it while you and Jones were taking down that barrier."

"What is it, NicAskill?" Mostyn asked.

"This way." She led Mostyn about thirty feet down the main tunnel, the rest of the team following.

"There, sir."

Lying on the floor next to the wall was a man curled up

under a blanket. His face was contorted into a mask of sheer terror.

Mostyn knelt and touched him. "Stone."

"Just like at the gallery," NicAskill said.

Mostyn stood. "Thanks, NicAskill."

"That means the Gorgon is down here, doesn't it, sir?" NicAskill asked.

"Makes sense," Mostyn said.

"Especially if, as you believe, Mr. Mostyn, the book is down here," Stoppen added.

"Okay, people. One more thing we need to keep an eye out for," Mostyn said. "Now let's go to Chinatown."

Mostyn walked back and entered the side tunnel, followed by his team. There was the sound of rats skittering away as the humans approached, along with the dripping of water. The air smelled stale and dank. There were no fans and no lights in this branch of the tunnel.

The floor was littered with broken chunks of concrete and many of the bricks comprising the walls had crumbled away, leaving a gritty powder on the floor.

Mostyn looked up. The beam of his helmet light revealed cracks and holes in the curved ceiling. He saw drops of water form in some of those cracks and holes and watched them as they fell to the floor.

"Will this tunnel take us all the way to Chinatown?" NicAskill asked.

"Not directly," Mostyn replied. "According to the map here, it looks like it will empty out into a spur of the old subway system."

"Are you sure?" Dr. Stoppen asked. "I'm not aware that

the Pacific Electric Railway ran into Chinatown. And the subway certainly didn't."

"Well something apparently did," Mostyn replied. "The map has a tunnel under Chinatown. See for yourself." And Mostyn motioned for Stoppen to take a look. "In addition, the guy I talked to in the Records Office mentioned a tunnel."

Stoppen shrugged. "What do I know? I'm just a librarian."

"Maybe these tunnels weren't dug by the city or the Pacific Electric Railway." NicAskill suggested.

"The lizard people are a myth," Stoppen shot back.

"Lizard people?" Jones said. "Lizard people in Los Angeles? Seriously?"

"There are no lizard people!" Stoppen fairly shouted the words.

"Not lizard people," NicAskill said. "I'm talking about secret federal government tunnels."

"You mean military tunnels," Jones said.

"That I do," NicAskill replied. "You know, Jonesy, you're pretty smart for a being a blond."

"You better hope I don't have to save your ass, Nicky. 'Cuz I just might think twice about it."

"No, you won't, Jonesy. All for one and one for all."

"Yeah, right."

"Okay, let's have some order here," Mostyn said. "It doesn't matter who made the tunnels. What does matter is that they'll get us close to Dr. Kemper, and, if I'm right, the book. Now keep your eyes and ears sharp. We're facing a dangerous enemy."

"I wonder if he used the lizard people to make those statues?" Jones said.

Mostyn shook his head. "Can it, Jones, and keep walking."

They covered another hundred feet, when, coming from the darkness ahead, they heard odd shambling sounds and a high-pitched tittering.

———

Dotty wanted to put her hands on her hips, but that wasn't possible. "Look here, Mr. Whatever-Your-Name-Is, why don't you let me go. Tell the boss man I escaped."

The man shook his head and returned to his chair.

"What do you get out of this?"

"I get nothing except knowing I served the master."

"My people can offer you more."

"I sincerely doubt that is possible, Dr. Kemper."

"Try me."

"No, thank you."

"All right, you lose."

Dotty turned around and walked to the wall into which the end of the chain was embedded. She tried wiggling it. Even though the wall was crumbling, the chain didn't budge. She gave the chain a good yank, but the wall mounting didn't give.

That isn't coming out anytime soon, she thought. *So now what?*

"Escape is futile," the man said.

"Blow it out your ass, buddy. Either help me, or shut up."

Dotty took one of the links of the chain and started scraping the wall around the mounting.

The man got up and stepped into the light.

"If you want to see how an escape artist works, you have to get closer."

The man said nothing.

Dotty yanked on the chain. "Ah, progress. I should be free in no time."

"I really must insist, Dr. Kemper, that you stop."

"Nope. Not going to."

From his pocket the man took out a vial and a syringe. From the corner of her eye, Dotty watched him take a measured amount of fluid from the vial. He then pocketed the vial and approached Dotty. He was as quiet as a cat.

Dotty continued working away and when she figured he was close enough, she spun around. Her left foot caught his right arm and the syringe catapulted out of his hand. With his left hand the man took a kubotan from his pocket. Dotty lashed out with her foot, and caught him in the crotch. The man doubled over and she kicked his head, sending him sprawling.

He was moaning, but not getting up. She grabbed his foot, pulled him to her, and wrapped the chain around his neck.

The man fought for a few moments and then went limp.

"Sorry, pal, but all's fair in love and war."

She unwrapped the chain from his neck and searched him for a key, but found nothing.

"Isn't that a fine how do you do?"

She caught sight of the kubotan and tried to get it, but it was just beyond her reach.

"Think, Dotty, think."

She looked at the man, took off one of his shoes, and used it to pull the kubotan closer to her.

"Now we're in business." She used the self-defense weapon to dig into the soft concrete. "By hook or by crook, I'm getting out of here."

18

DOTTY KEMPER GAVE the chain a yank, and pulled it partially free from the wall. She gave it another tug and it pulled free.

"All right, Kemper, now you're cooking," she said to herself. "Grab that lantern and get the hell out of here."

Before she did, however, she checked her dead guard once more for a set of keys and any weapons. He had neither, save for the kubotan, syringe, and vial. Dotty pocketed all three and took stock of where she was.

Holding the lantern high, she saw she was in an alcove, or a wide area of the tunnel. The tunnel itself, she noticed, was old and seemed to be at least partially carved out of rock. The concrete and brick portions were in desperate need of repair.

"Don't sneeze, Dotty," she told herself. "You just might bring the whole thing crashing down on top of you."

She looked right and then left. The feeble light of the lantern seemed to be swallowed up in the darkness.

"Six of one and half a dozen of the other," she muttered, and with a shrug she turned to her left and began walking, staying close to the wall on her right.

The stone was dry and showed evidence it had once had a coating of cement that was now gone. *Probably the grit I'm walking on*, she mused.

About five hundred paces in, she noticed the tunnel began angling down and became noticeably damp. At spots water could be seen running down the wall in tiny rivulets.

"Maybe going left wasn't such a good idea," she muttered.

Another five hundred paces and she found her way blocked. The tunnel had collapsed and water lay stagnant at the base of the rubble.

"Okay, Dotty, going left got you nowhere," she said to the tunnel walls. "Let's backtrack and go the other direction."

She retraced her steps, passed the alcove where she'd been held prisoner, and continued on down the tunnel. After walking several hundred paces past the alcove, she came across a tunnel entrance closed off with iron bars. She paused a moment, before holding up the lantern, but the feeble light revealed little.

"Sure wish I could get out of these manacles," she muttered. "They're really cramping my style."

She grabbed hold of one of the bars, and tried yanking on it, but it didn't budge, and she continued walking down the tunnel.

After a time, and about a thousand paces, she came to a

Y. The tunnel she was following continued on, bearing slightly to the right. Another tunnel came in from the left.

She stopped and considered her options. Neither tunnel was illuminated, and the lantern revealed little. Both tunnels were level, or seemed to be, and thereby gave no indication as to which one would take her to the surface. That is, if either one did, in fact, go to the surface.

"I could be wandering around down here until I die of thirst," she muttered.

With a shrug, Dotty Kemper pushed on ahead. The tunnel, after a hundred or so feet, curved to the right. Dotty followed it, wondering where she actually was in Los Angeles.

Up ahead she saw beams of light illuminating the wall, bouncing slightly up and down, and heard a soft whine, as from an electric motor.

The tunnel must curve to the left up there, she thought.

And in a moment, six pairs of lights rounded the curve and stopped. Dotty was bathed in light and there was nowhere for her to hide.

"Well, well, well, if it isn't the ever resourceful Dr. Kemper." The voice was softly sibilant, and seemed to echo off the walls. It also sounded very old. Yet very much fraught with menace.

"I guess you found me, Mr. Masked Man," Dotty replied.

"And that is a good thing," the masked man said, "because you and I have some work we need to do."

———

The shambling and tittering sounds were slowly and steadily growing louder. Mostyn softly called Jones's and NicAskill's names, and told the rest of his team to stay back. From out of his backpack, Jones took a couple of grenades. Out of NicAskill's backpack came the parts from which she assembled a small thermobaric grenade launcher.

"Everybody get down," Mostyn said. He, Jones, and NicAskill got into prone shooting positions.

"This floor is disgusting," Dr. Winifred Petrie said just before she was whisked off her feet. Her screams filled the air as she flew towards the darkness that lay before the team.

"What the hell's going on?" Jones said.

While Petrie's cries became weaker and her struggles gradually ceased, a blood red amorphous obscenity gradually came into view.

"Oh my God!" Dr. Stoppen cried out, pointing at the alien being. "It's a star vampire!"

Jones opened fire with his forty-five, the bullets having no visible effect on the tittering monstrosity that was before them.

The tentacled amoeboid blasphemy of Newton's Laws dropped the shriveled husk that was once Dr. Petrie. The entirety of the enormous thing was now visible, glowing a brilliant blood red.

NicAskill took aim and fired a thermobaric grenade at the creature. The missile passed through the oncoming amorphous blob and exploded behind the thing. The heat and pressure wave scorched and flattened the unholy tittering malevolence from another dimension. It's blood red color turned black.

Reloading and taking aim, NicAskill fired a second grenade. The projectile flew mere inches above the tunnel floor and again passed through the creature, exploding when it hit the tunnel wall. Intense heat, pressure, and flames turned the amoeboid thing to ash, the monster's insane titters turning to ear piercing shrieks as it burned to death.

When there was only the crackling of the flames as they consumed the last of the alien flesh, Mostyn and his team members got to their feet.

"What the hell was that thing?" Jones asked.

"Stoppen said it was a star vampire," NicAskill said, "whatever the hell that is."

Dr. Stoppen shrieked, "He must have *De Vermis Mysteriis*. We are undone!"

Mostyn turned to look at Stoppen. "Otto, get a grip."

Stoppen began to visibly shake. "We are doomed!" the librarian screamed.

Mostyn went up to him, took hold of his shoulders, and shook him. Hard. "Get a hold of yourself, man. We have a mission."

"But, but..."

Mostyn shook the man again. "All the more reason to get this guy. Right?"

There was no response from Stoppen.

Mostyn shook him again. The man was like a rag doll. "Am I right, Dr. Stoppen? We have to stop him!"

Stoppen seemed to come back to life. "Yes, yes. We must stop him. He is too dangerous."

Mostyn took hold of the librarian's shoulders, looked him in the eyes, and said, "You're okay?"

Stoppen nodded. "Yes, yes, I'm okay, Mostyn. Had a bad experience with a star vampire some years ago. Some things don't leave you."

"No, they don't, Otto. But this one's dead, and it isn't going to hurt anyone else."

Stoppen nodded, took a deep breath, and exhaled before speaking. "Yes, I'm okay. Ready to complete this mission."

"Good." Mostyn turned to everyone else. "Okay, people, let's go."

The tunnel began to shake and pieces of concrete fell to the floor, bounced, and came to a stop.

"This doesn't look good, Mostyn," Baker called out. "The blasts must have destabilized the tunnel."

"Everybody, double time," Mostyn yelled.

"We're going in there?" Hammerschmidt said.

"Get going," Mostyn yelled. "Before a concrete cairn marks your resting place."

The six remaining team members charged ahead, running full tilt into the trembling tunnel. Chunks of concrete pelted them as they ran. A large chunk narrowly missed Mostyn and a smaller one hit Jones's backpack, making him stumble. NicAskill grabbed him to keep him from falling.

Hammerschmidt wasn't so lucky. The chemist was knocked to the floor when a large piece of the ceiling fell on him. Baker hauled him to his feet and called for help.

Jones dropped back and picked the doctor up in a fireman's carry.

The tunnel was shaking violently, making it difficult for Mostyn and his team to remain on their feet.

"We're not going to make it, Boss," NicAskill yelled, just before a tremor knocked her off her feet.

Mostyn grabbed her under her arms and dragged her to the side of the tunnel.

"Everyone!" Mostyn yelled and motioned for them to take a protective position along the tunnel wall.

The team hunkered down, facing the wall, all curled into fetal positions, their backs and backpacks positioned outward. There was a roar as tons of concrete and bricks came cascading down from the ceiling and walls.

————

Dotty Kemper opened her eyes. Above her was an arched ceiling.

Must still be in this goddamn tunnel, she thought.

Slowly she sat up and looked around. This portion of the tunnel was in a remarkably good state of repair. The lights, while not bright, provided adequate illumination.

"Well, I'll be damned," she said out loud. "A bed. I'm sitting on a bed."

And as she took in where she was, she realized she was in a room. There were walls and a door and a few pieces of furniture.

"Huh. They must've converted a section of the tunnel into apartments," Dotty muttered.

She got off the bed and walked to the door. After examining it to check for wiring that might trigger an alarm, she tried the doorknob. Locked. A look of disgust flitted across her face.

Dotty walked around the room. *What are they going to do with me?* she thought. *If they were just going to kill me they would have done so by now.*

She opened the wardrobe, and counted eight dresses. In the drawers, were underclothes.

At least I'll look pretty, she thought.

Dotty returned to the bed and sat on it. "I'm awake, Mr. Masked Man," she called out. "How about you tell me what the program is?"

There was a knock, and the sound of the lock clicking. The door opened outward and a woman walked in. She pulled the door closed behind her. Kemper noticed the lock did not click, which meant for the time being she wasn't locked in.

Dotty studied the woman. She was Chinese and looked like she was maybe in her late twenties or early thirties. She was wearing a red cheongsam, with a white floral print. The dress had long side slits, and a high collar. The sleeves came to the midpoint of her forearms. Her hair was black and cut short. She wore red lipstick and her long fingernails were painted red.

"My name's Dotty. What's yours?"

"My name does not matter." The English was perfect. The accent American Midwest. "But you may call me *Zi*. I am to prepare you."

"Prepare me for what?"

"The master will enlighten you soon. Please do not resist, or attempt to hurt me. Precautions have been taken."

"Precautions?" Dotty said, and launched herself at the young woman, whose black eyes turned red, and Dotty found herself sprawled on the floor. She felt as though she'd run full tilt into a brick wall. She slowly picked herself up off the floor.

"Yes. Precautions," Dotty said.

"I told you precautions had been taken."

Dotty shook her head. "So you did."

"Now, shall we begin? The master is waiting, and he does not like to be kept waiting."

19

PIERCE MOSTYN slowly opened his eyes and coughed. He gradually maneuvered himself into a sitting position. He was covered in a grayish-colored dust and bits of concrete, brick, and earth. He looked at the humps of dust and dirt that marked where his team members lay, and slowly stood.

The last one in the line was only a few feet from where a wall of broken masonry and earth stretched from floor to ceiling. Mostyn made his way to that last team member and shook him. The person was Willie Lee Baker.

"Willie Lee, are you okay?" Mostyn shook him again.

A groan came from his lips, and Mostyn brushed away the stones and dirt. "Are you okay, Willie Lee?"

Baker shook his head and opened his eyes.

"Are you all right?"

"Yeah, I think so, Mostyn. I'm not in any great pain."

"Good to hear."

Mostyn moved down the row checking on each team

member. They were all alive. Hammerschmidt's back hurt, and NicAskill complained about her thigh. But there were no broken bones. Mostyn breathed a sigh of relief.

"Listen up," he began, "we can only move forward. Somewhere ahead of us are Dr. Kemper and the book, and perhaps more unpleasant surprises. Drink some water, clear your heads, and get ready to move out."

Mostyn took out his phone and brought up the holographic map of the tunnel system. The first thing he noticed was the dot representing Dotty Kemper had moved. He keyed his helmet mic.

"Sumer Base. Come in, Sumer Base."

"We read you, Mostyn, but you're breaking up."

"Same for you, Langston. We had a cave-in."

"Anyone hurt?"

"We lost Petrie, but not in the cave-in. Our adversary had a star vampire hiding down here."

"Good God. Sorry to hear about Petrie. She was a valuable asset."

"Thanks. And yes, she was. I notice Dr. Kemper's moved. Where is she now?"

"She's under central Chinatown. Before that she was under a church. I've highlighted the most direct route for you to reach her. You should see it on the hologram now."

"Roger that, Sumer Base."

"Mostyn, we've..."

The transmission disintegrated into static.

"Jones, anything you can do with the phone?"

"No, Boss. Maybe we need to get clear of this cave-in. It might be interfering with reception."

"Okay, let's move out. We need to quick time it." And Mostyn took off at a jog down the tunnel, the rest of the team following. Behind Mostyn was Baker, and behind him were Stoppen, NicAskill, Hammerschmidt, and Jones.

A half-mile down the tunnel a side branch came in, and Mostyn took it. He continued on for five hundred feet and stopped.

"According to my calculations, we have at least a mile, maybe two, to go before we reach Dr. Kemper. I'm going to divide the team. NicAskill and I are going to go on ahead."

"And we slowpokes," Dr. Stoppen said, "will catch up as soon as possible."

"No offense, Dr. Stoppen," Mostyn said.

"None taken, Special Agent Mostyn. Go rescue Dr. Kemper and secure the book. We'll catch up as soon as we can."

"Sure you don't need a photographer?" Baker asked.

"Sorry, Willie Lee," Mostyn replied.

"Okay, I can take a hint," Baker said, with a smile. "I need to go on a diet."

"Your words, not mine," Mostyn said.

Baker waved away Mostyn's comment. "Yeah, yeah. You just want NicAskill to yourself."

Mostyn simply smiled, and turned to Jones. "Keep everyone safe." He had Jones study the hologram and the route he'd need to follow.

"Okay, NicAskill, let's go."

The two sprinted down the tunnel and quickly disappeared into the Stygian blackness.

Dr. Dotty Kemper took a look at herself in the mirror Zi had provided her. She'd bathed in an old-fashioned tin tub that had been brought in. She'd been given a massage. Zi had expertly applied her makeup.

I look pretty damn good, Dotty thought. To Zi, she said, "So what's all this for?"

"The master will tell you. He will come soon." Zi turned and left. Men came in and removed the tub and the mirror. On their departure, the door was closed and locked.

Dotty sat in a chair. "Well, Mr. Masked Man," she said out loud, "you're either getting me all dolled up for my wedding or my funeral. And if it's my funeral, then I guess I'm going out with a bang."

After a moment, her flippant attitude vanished. "I don't want to die." The words came out soft and barely audible. "I don't want to be some monster's baby factory either. I want to be with Pierce. I want him to hold me, and kiss me, and make love to me, and treat me like a princess." Tears collected in her eyes, and then ran down her cheeks.

Mostyn and NicAskill ran down the tunnel. The beams from their helmet lamps bounced off the walls and floor. Rubble was everywhere. A testimony to the deterioration of the abandoned tunnel.

Phone in hand, Mostyn kept them on course, moving ever closer to Dotty Kemper's location.

"Take that tunnel there," Mostyn said.

He and NicAskill turned down a tunnel that came in on their right. However, fifty feet in the hologram collapsed and disappeared.

"Oh for crying out loud," Mostyn exclaimed.

"What, Boss?"

"The hologram collapsed. Either my phone is dead, or we are out of range of Jones's special phone. Mostyn tried contacting Sumer Base and was greeted with nothing but static.

"Looks like we're out of range," NicAskill said.

"It does. But the map should be in the app and shouldn't be dependent on a connection to Sumer Base."

"Well, whatever it is, we don't have it. So now what?"

Mostyn pulled a compass out of a pocket. "She was north and east. We keep going."

They ran for another four hundred feet and came to a stop. The tunnel disappeared into a dark opening. Mostyn walked to the edge. He looked up. Nothing but darkness beyond the reach of his helmet lamp. He lay on the floor, and peered over the edge into the incredible blackness. He closed his eyes and swallowed, forcing down the bile rising in his throat. He took deep breaths to quell the vertigo threatening to overwhelm him.

He opened his eyes and took another look. Nothing but darkness stretched beyond the reach of the lamp. He pushed himself back from the edge and stood up.

"A vertical shaft" he announced. "The tunnel ends in a vertical shaft."

NicAskill walked to the edge and dropped a piece of

rubble. After a couple seconds they heard it hit something solid.

"An elevator shaft?" NicAskill asked.

"Maybe. The question is, how do we get down?"

"You sure we want to go down and not up?"

"Not one hundred percent sure, but if I were our masked man, I'd hold Dotty in a lower tunnel, not a higher one. Less chance of her being found in a lower tunnel."

"Makes sense, Boss." NicAskill swept the shaft wall opposite them with her lamp. "Over there is a ladder." She pointed. "See? Along the wall?"

"And it has to be over there rather than over here." Mostyn shook his head.

He and NicAskill slipped off their backpacks, rummaged inside, and pulled out abseil lines and small grappling hooks. They each attached a grappling hook to one end of a line.

"All set?" Mostyn asked.

"Ready to go."

"Very good. Ladies first."

NicAskill tossed the grappling hook across the expanse of the shaft. It caught on one of the rungs. She pulled on the line. Both the hook and ladder held. She sat on the edge, drew in a deep breath, and scooted off. Through the air she sailed, her boots hit the wall on either side of the ladder. She bounced back a ways, came back in, and grabbed the ladder with her left hand. She let go of the line.

"Seems sturdy enough," she called back to Mostyn.

She climbed a few rungs, retrieved the grappling hook and started down the ladder.

Mostyn repeated what NicAskill had done and in a few minutes both were in the lower tunnel.

"I don't think this is part of the original system," NicAskill said.

"Or maybe it is the original system."

The tunnel was narrow, at most three people could stand side by side. The ceiling was only about seven feet above the floor. The walls and ceiling were rough hewn stone. The floor had been smoothed in places with concrete. Mostyn figured that had been a more recent addition.

The lighting fixtures were few and far between and were not operating. They were located along the wall near the ceiling.

"God, it's hotter than hell down here," NicAskill said.

"No ventilation either," Mostyn added. He looked at the compass. "At least it goes in the same general direction we want to go."

The two packed up the grapnels and abseil lines, put them in each other's backpacks, and took off down the tunnel. About a thousand feet on, the tunnel made a sharp turn to the left. Mostyn and NicAskill came to a quick stop. For standing before them were two creatures.

"Oh, my God!" NicAskill exclaimed. "The lizard people!"

20

THE MAN with the mask sat in a chair that had been carried in by the same two beautiful young women who had carried it in to Dotty's prison suite. They stood behind him. She noticed one had a very nice looking bruise on her face, and gave her a smile. The woman didn't acknowledge her.

"I have decided," the ancient softly sibilant voice said, "that you would not make a good daughter-in-law. Nor would you make a good mother for my great-grandchildren. Therefore there will be no marriage. Nor do I wish to simply extract information from your mind and then kill you. That would be a waste of a very useful human life."

He looked at Dotty, and she looked back at him; straight at the eyes behind the mask, and said nothing.

The masked man met her gaze. "That leaves me with two alternatives: extract the information you have and then either turn you into a zuvembie and use you to foil those who seek to learn of me, or use you to unlock the gate. The question that must be answered is whether or not now is the best time to open the gate."

"And what happens if you open the gate?" Dotty asked.

"You cannot see, Dr. Kemper, but you have made me smile."

"How nice."

"Do you remember the statues of Mr. Cortado?"

"Yes."

"They came from me. You might say that I'm the agent for the true artist."

"And who, or I should say what, is the true artist?"

"You are a fast learner, Dr. Kemper. The true artist is not of this universe, or even of this dimension. Many millennia ago they came to this world, the Terrible Ones, for that is what Gorgon means in ancient Greek. They were deemed immortal because the ancients did not possess the means to slay them. Eventually they passed into Greek myth. The infamous Medusa and her sisters."

"As I remember the story, Medusa got her head cut off."

"True. That was only after her Achilles heel, as it were, was discovered. Up until then, the Gorgons were invincible."

"So they're mortal just like you and me."

"I'm smiling again. More like you, than me. However, that is all by the by. Now, thanks to *Die unaussprechlichen Riten von dem dessen Name nicht genannt werden Kann*, I have been able to bring one of the Gorgons to this world. Sacrificing you, for you are physically not unlike the ancient Greeks, will let me summon a whole host of these beings, who are part of the vanguard of the Great Old

Ones themselves. The dawning of this universe's night is nigh!"

"And what's in it for you? Why are you excluded from being lunch meat?"

"Because the book also gives me the incantation that grants me protection. I will be the only human to rule over my puny race with Azathoth, Nyarlathotep, Shub-Niggurath, Chaugnar Faugn, and Cthulhu Himself!"

"You're deluded. And because of you, we're all — including you — going to end up being appetizers at the most hideous banquet of all time."

"I know one thing, Dr. Kemper, if I decide to open the gate, *you* will not be on the menu."

———

The scene was like a tableau in a wax museum. Mostyn and NicAskill on one side and the two humanoid creatures on the other. All four standing stock still. And then Mostyn and NicAskill drew their pistols, at the same time the creatures emitted a high-pitched sound that shattered the helmet lamps plunging the tunnel into darkness. By the time Mostyn found his flashlight and turned it on, the creatures were gone.

"My God, Boss, the lizard people. We've seen the lizard people!"

"Looks that way, NicAskill." Mostyn took a wrist flashlight out of his backpack. "Get yours on and let's keep moving."

NicAskill put her flashlight on her wrist and, once

again, the two OUP agents took off running down the tunnel. After a couple thousand feet, the tunnel they were in emptied into a larger tunnel, which still had rails embedded into the floor. Mostyn noticed up above, the wire for the power to the electric train.

He consulted the compass. "If we go left, that should take us into Chinatown."

"Where's this Medusa creature?" NicAskill asked.

"Don't know. However, now that you mention it…" Mostyn rummaged in his backpack, and pulled out a mirror.

"Bardon thinks of everything," NicAskill said, as she took out her mirror. "They're not very big."

"They aren't. We'll have to make do."

"I guess so. Otherwise we'll be decorations in some-one's foyer."

"If we're that lucky. Come on." And Mostyn took off running down the tunnel, with NicAskill following.

"Are bullets going to kill this thing?" NicAskill asked.

"Perseus used a sword. The trick is being able to kill it without looking at it. Perseus was lucky. Medusa was asleep and he had a hat that made him invisible."

"I think Bardon forgot that part."

"Maybe he has more confidence in us than the gods had in Perseus."

"That's one way to look at it," NicAskill said, although her face wasn't so optimistic.

The two OUP agents ran down the tunnel, and by Mostyn's guess moved deeper into the world beneath Chinatown. After half a mile they stopped. Before them the tunnel divided into three branches. The rails and electric wire continued on in the tunnel that bore to the right.

"Now what, Boss?"

"Good question. And I don't have a good answer." Mostyn thought a moment, shrugged, and pointed to the left tunnel. "Let's see where that one goes."

They entered and jogged for about a hundred feet before the floor began to angle upwards.

Mostyn came to a stop. "This one's going to the surface, let's go back."

They retraced their steps and returned to the spot where the four tunnels came together.

"Okay, NicAskill, fifty-fifty. Which one?"

"Let's take the center tunnel."

"The center one it is."

They jogged down the center tunnel and after a couple hundred feet, the passage began to descend.

"Remind me not to play poker with you."

NicAskill let out a laugh. "I don't gamble, sir."

"You're in the OUP, what do you call that?"

"A calculated risk, sir."

Mostyn laughed. "That it is, NicAskill. That it is."

After another couple hundred feet, the tunnel walls changed from concrete to stone, and the curved ceiling became flat. The stone was rough hewn, except for the floor, which was fairly smooth. Mostyn noted the walls were dry. The air was hot and stale. There was also no indication that there had ever been electric wiring in the tunnel.

"This must be very old, Boss."

"Looks that way."

"I wonder if the lizard people made this."

"Possibly. May have been Native Americans."

"What for?"

"Who knows? Maybe someplace to hide from us."

"Why did you decide to continue following this tunnel, sir?"

"Just a guess. The other was going up. This one isn't. As I said before, if I were the masked man, I'd take Dr. Kemper lower, not higher. To keep her from being found."

"Makes sense, sir. Just hope we find her."

"Me, too, NicAskill. Me too."

21
_____

DOTTY KEMPER LAY on the bed. The masked man had left her, left her in order to determine her fate.

"I'm going to die," she muttered. "He is going to either sacrifice me or turn me into some kind of mindless thing to do his bidding. In either case I'll be dead." Dotty took a deep breath and exhaled. "I wonder if he'll grant me a last wish?"

She had no idea of the time. No idea how long the masked man had been gone. No idea if Mostyn was looking for her.

She snorted. "Of course he's looking for me. Probably with half an army. He loves me." And for a moment Dotty Kemper took comfort in that thought. If she was going to die, at least she'd die knowing she was loved.

She sat up on the bed, and looked at the door. Locked. She'd tried it after the masked man had left. She got up and went to the door, trying it again.

"Still locked," she muttered. "Too bad I never had

Helene teach me how to dematerialize. Would never have been in this situation to begin with."

Dotty sighed and returned to the bed, where she sat facing the door. The room was clear of things she could use for weapons. She was completely on her own. She was going to die. That's all there was to it.

She heard the click and watched the door open. Before her was the Chinese woman whose eyes had turned red, the one who called herself *Zi*, and the masked man.

He began speaking without any preamble. "I have made my decision. Tonight the moon is full. Your sacrifice tonight will open the gate which will allow the Gorgons to enter this dimension, making straight the path for the Great Old Ones to follow. Zi will extract the information that is in your mind, and then you'll be readied for the sacrifice. You must be prepared so you are acceptable to them."

The masked man departed. The door closed and the tell-tale click announced the door was locked.

The two women looked at each other. Dotty spoke. "Do you actually want him to unleash a horror that will destroy this planet? Do you want to die?"

Zi, her face registering no emotion, said, "I will not die, for I am not human."

Suddenly it all made sense. "Of course. Precautions."

"Precisely. Precautions. Now, Dr Kemper, lie down upon the bed."

"No."

"Very well."

Dotty watched Zi lift her arm and point a finger at her.

Immediately she felt all the strength go out of her body, and felt herself fall back onto the bed. Dotty realized she was completely helpless. Completely at the mercy of the alien woman. In her mind she laughed a mirthless laugh. Mercy. She was not going to get any mercy.

All Dotty could do was watch the Chinese-looking woman lay her on her back and position her limbs and torso. It was as though Dotty was nothing more than a rag doll.

When she was apparently positioned just right, the alien got on the bed and straddled Dotty, placing her fingertips on Dotty's head.

Unable to squirm or scream or even blink, Dotty felt as though a vacuum cleaner was running over her mind.

———

Mostyn stopped. He needed a five minute rest. As fit as he was, age was beginning its little tell-tale signs. He looked at NicAskill. While she appreciated the rest, she didn't need it. He sipped from his canteen, and his partner did likewise.

The tunnel, after descending for at least half a mile had ended. Terminating in a staircase that led deeper into the earth below the city.

NicAskill peered into the blackness. Her wrist light revealed nothing but stairs. "I wonder who built these? I don't think Native Americans would. What could possibly be their reason? On the other hand, the lizard people... Do you think they built this?"

Mostyn shrugged. "Your guess is as good as mine. I just hope these take us to Dotty."

"Do you think the others are going to catch up?"

"Don't know. Hopefully they will, sooner rather than later."

Mostyn took one last swallow of water, put the canteen away, and indicated it was time to descend.

Down the stairs they went, Mostyn in the lead. The stairwell had been carved out of solid stone. The steps, carved from the same stone, were worn in the center.

"At one time these steps had a lot of use," NicAskill said.

"Given the dust, I'd say that was a long time ago."

"Yeah. A very long time ago. This stuff has to be at least an inch thick."

"And no footprints. So we're the first to come this way in a long time."

The stairwell was free of decorations. Nothing but the chiseled rock. The temperature gradually became cooler the further they descended, and after a time the stone changed from dry to wet.

From behind him, Mostyn heard NicAskill curse.

"What's the matter?"

"Ugh. I don't like the wet and the slime."

"Just pray we aren't dumped into an underground lake or river when this thing ends."

NicAskill groaned.

The stairs continued for another fifty or sixty feet and came to an end in another tunnel. The floor was wet with a film of standing water. The walls were water-slicked and slime covered.

They had followed the tunnel for a hundred feet or so when Mostyn and NicAskill found themselves at an intersection. They were in a small chamber which four other tunnels fed into.

Mostyn shook his head. "Can this get any harder?" he muttered. He pointed. "Go to that tunnel and listen. Tell me if you hear anything. I'll start with this one. We'll meet in the middle."

NicAskill went to her tunnel and walked in a few paces and listened. Mostyn did the same with his tunnel. Not hearing a sound, save for dripping water, he went back out to the little chamber. There he saw NicAskill, who shook her head, and went into the next tunnel. Mostyn did likewise.

Almost immediately Mostyn noticed a slight incline to the floor. The tunnel was also fairly dry. He stopped about twenty feet from the entrance and listened. Chanting! He heard chanting!

He ran out. NicAskill was waiting.

"Come! Listen!"

Mostyn pulled her to the spot where he'd been standing. "Listen," he said.

"Sounds like some kind of singing."

"Chanting," Mostyn said. "Come on. Let's go. Keep your weapons handy — and your mirror."

They ran down the tunnel making as little noise as possible, the chanting gradually growing louder the further into the tunnel they progressed. After a few hundred feet, Mostyn put his hand up and stopped.

"What is it?" NicAskill whispered.

"Light. Up there." Mostyn turned off his wrist light.

Perhaps fifty feet in front of them they saw a rectangular entryway and the dull glow of light coming from beyond.

They crept forward and passed through the opening. Mostyn looked around. They appeared to be on a balcony, carved from the solid rock. A short wall about three feet high ran around the edge of the balcony. There was a set of stairs on one side that Mostyn assumed led down to the floor below.

He got down on all fours. The chanting was quite loud now, and seemed to be building towards a climax. There was no source of light higher up in the chamber, and Mostyn assumed the light they were seeing must be coming from down below. He crept to the edge of the balcony and peered over the wall. About thirty feet below was a large auditorium. A group of a couple dozen men were dressed in long robes and chanting. The words were now audible and they were all too familiar to Mostyn.

"C'goka fahf tgif ng ymg'uln. O n ghft ehye."

NicAskill hunkered down beside Mostyn, and whispered, "What are they singing?"

"I don't know. But whatever it is, it can't be good. It's R'lyehian. And I've never been anywhere where that language was a good sign. Look."

NicAskill looked to where Mostyn was pointing. On a raised semi-circular dais, four naked women were holding down another naked woman who was spread eagle on a large flat stone, which was obviously an altar. Each of the women were squatting and holding one of the limbs of the woman lying spread eagle on the stone.

A man was standing next to the altar, holding a large knife in the air, his face elevated towards the ceiling, and his mouth was moving. Perhaps in some invocation.

NicAskill gasped. "Oh, my God, Boss. That's Dr. Kemper!"

22

MOSTYN SHRUGGED out of his backpack, took out a stun grenade, and hurled it onto the dais. The flash-bang caused instant pandemonium. Mostyn and NicAskill charged down the steps that led from the balcony to the main floor, across the auditorium, and up the steps to the dais.

The women who had been holding Dotty were screaming their panic at being unable to see or hear. The man with the knife had vanished.

Mostyn picked up Dotty, who looked as though she'd been drugged, and headed back towards the steps leading up to the balcony.

A couple of the men who had been chanting tried blocking Mostyn's way and were shot down by NicAskill. Up the stairs the three went, and once on the balcony, Mostyn laid Dotty down and tried to rouse her. NicAskill dispatched two more of the men in the long robes as they climbed the stairs.

"Can you get her awake, Boss?"

"She's pretty much out of it. Keeps mumbling something about a Chinese woman, but I can't make out the words."

"We're going to have to get a move on, they're getting ready to mount a counterattack."

"All right, then, let's get a move on." Mostyn slipped on his backpack and hoisted Dotty up over his shoulder and moved into the tunnel.

NicAskill fired a thermobaric grenade into the auditorium and then joined Mostyn. "That ought to slow them down, Boss."

"Take the lead, NicAskill."

"I can help carry her."

"No, one of us needs to be ready for action."

"Yes, sir." NicAskill moved past Mostyn, taking the lead, as they walked down the tunnel.

Two men appeared in the tunnel entrance, and NicAskill dropped them before they got off a shot. She sprinted ahead and at the tunnel entrance, Mostyn saw gun flashes and heard the firearm reports. He carefully lay Dotty down, and once again tried to rouse her. All he got was incoherent mumbling about the Chinese woman.

Mostyn stood and saw NicAskill hurl a grenade. The explosion was deafening in the confined world of the tunnel. And even where he was standing, his ears were ringing.

NicAskill yelled, "All clear for the moment," and moved out into the intersection of the five tunnels.

Mostyn picked up Dotty and followed NicAskill into the

intersection of the tunnels, where he saw they were surrounded by armed men in black suits.

———

It hadn't taken DC Jones long to figure out that Mostyn and NicAskill would soon be out of range and he'd lose contact with them. He made a call to Sumer Base and managed to relay through the static that Langston needed to send him the holographic map he'd sent to Mostyn. Langston sent the map and now Jones had the tunnel system and also the little blinking dots from the sub-dermal trackers showing where Dotty, Mostyn, and NicAskill were in the pile of spaghetti that was the tunnel system below Los Angeles.

Dr. Otto Stoppen was the slowest moving in the group, which frustrated Jones to no end, as the doctor's slowness prevented the team from making good time. However, with Langston's guidance, Jones's group was able to take a couple shortcuts that got them into Chinatown fairly quickly.

"Jones," Langston began, "now that you're under Chinatown, we're going to be dependent on your eyes and ears. Our maps are close to non-existent for this part of the tunnel system."

"Roger that, Langston," Jones replied, and began a running monologue of the tunnels as they passed through.

Fifteen or so minutes into the monologue, Jones said, "Okay, we're coming up to a ninety degree left turn." There was a brief pause, before Jones continued, "I've made the turn. There's another tunnel coming in at a right angle... What the hell?"

Baker snapped a picture, at the same time saying, "Oh, my God, it's the lizard people!"

Everyone came to a halt. In the tunnel joining the one Jones and the team were in, were four strange-looking beings. They were humanoid in form. Their skin appeared to have the texture of a lizard's, and their heads were block-shaped, with the jaw protruding somewhat. They had two slits instead of a nose, and their ears were small and lay flat to the head. The creatures appeared to have no hair, and they wore no clothes.

Jones regained his composure first. He held up his hands, and said, "We won't hurt you. We're looking for our friends."

Two of the creatures looked at each other, then turned back to Jones. Into his mind popped images of Mostyn and NicAskill.

"Yes, yes!" Jones said, and smiled.

Next came an image of Dotty Kemper.

"Yes!" Jones said, and once again smiled.

A fourth image came into Jones's mind, that of the masked man.

Jones shook his head, put on an angry face, and said, "No! He's not our friend."

The two creatures faced each other for some time, then one turned to Jones and in Jones's mind a picture of him and the team following the creatures.

Jones smiled in reply and said, "Yes."

"What's going on down there, Jones?" Langston asked.

"Just made contact with the lizard people."

"Lizard people? Are you serious?"

"Yep. Baker even snapped a pic. The lizard people know about Mostyn, NicAskill, and Kemper. If I understand them correctly, they're going to take us to them."

"Sounds too good to be true."

"We'll find out."

"You sure they aren't a product of sewer gas? You know, you're imagining them?"

Jones chuckled. "We'll find out soon enough."

The team followed the lizard people down the tunnel. The passageway made several turns and after the last one Jones saw light and heard voices, voices he recognized. The voices of Pierce Mostyn and Kymbra NicAskill.

———

"We're a bit outgunned, Boss," NicAskill said, "so what's our game plan?"

"I thought you said it was all clear?"

"It was when I said it. So now what?"

Before Mostyn could answer, from out of one of the tunnels stepped the masked man. Next to him was a beautiful Chinese woman.

"Special Agent in Charge Pierce Mostyn, we meet again," the masked man said in his ethereally sibilant voice. "Although you and your Dr. Bardon did have me fooled. However, my accomplice," he turned and gave a slight nod to the Chinese woman, "was able to extract much useful information from Dr. Kemper. Now I know who you are and what you want. Unfortunately for you, you and Dr. Bardon will not succeed this time."

The masked man motioned with his hand and two men stepped up to Mostyn and took Dotty Kemper from him. As they were doing so, Dotty muttered, "Chinese woman, bad."

"The conflagration you unleashed in my temple, Special Agent NicAskill, only delays the inevitable. However, I will now have you to sacrifice with Dr. Kemper which will ensure my success."

The masked man made a movement with his hand and two men approached NicAskill. At that moment, a high-pitched cry, almost outside the range of human hearing, sounded, the bulbs in the flashlights and lanterns burst, and the tunnel went black.

23

MOSTYN HIT THE FLOOR, and took out his pistol. He saw light in the entryway of one of the tunnels, and then gunfire erupted.

Jones, Mostyn thought. *Hallelujah!*

Arcing through the air were two flares. They hit the wall and fell to the floor. The bright light illuminated the situation in the small chamber. Mostyn's eyes swept the room. He spotted two men struggling to drag Dotty from the chamber.

He fired a double-tap from his pistol, sending two forty-five caliber bullets into one of the men. The man pitched forward as if he'd been hit with a sledgehammer. The other man let go of Dotty, turned around, and fell backwards under the impact from another pair of bullets sent by Mostyn's pistol.

With pistol in one hand and knife in the other, Mostyn low crawled across the floor to where Dotty lay. When he reached her, he positioned himself in front of her and took in the scene. Several of the black suits lay dead and there was no sign of the masked man or the Chinese woman. Jones, Baker, Hammerschmidt, and Stoppen entered the chamber. NicAskill stood up, her knife blade colored red.

Dotty groaned, and muttered, "Chinese woman. Stop her."

Mostyn touched her cheek, stood, and said, "That tunnel," he pointed to the one he meant, "the masked man and the Chinese woman were there. Let's go."

"Wait a minute," Jones said, "where are the lizard people?"

"You saw them too?" NicAskill said.

"They led us here," Jones replied.

"Well, I'll be...," NicAskill muttered.

"Let's go!" Mostyn shouted. "Jones, NicAskill, you first. And when you see the masked man or the Chinese-looking woman that was with him, shoot first, ask questions later."

"Right, Boss," Jones said, and plunged into the tunnel, with NicAskill following.

"Baker, Hammerschmidt, you two help Dotty."

"My God, Mostyn, she's in her birthday suit," Baker said, dropping his pack and stripping off his shirt.

"Thanks, Willie Lee," Mostyn replied, and to Dr. Stoppen he said, "Follow me!"

Mostyn and Stoppen plunged into the tunnel. Almost immediately Mostyn noticed the tunnel descended deeper into the earth.

Maybe this connects to the auditorium, he thought.

Jones and NicAskill were about fifty feet ahead of Mostyn. They ran around a curve in the tunnel, and a moment later Mostyn, significantly ahead of Stoppen, rounded the curve and almost ran into Jones, who'd stopped.

Before them stood the Chinese-looking woman. Her hand was raised in a signal to halt. "The master says, good-bye. It is time for you to die."

Her eyes turned red and she began to change shape.

"She's the Gorgon!" Mostyn yelled, Dotty's words suddenly making sense. The three OUP agents opened fire with their pistols. The Gorgon's body shook and twisted under the impact of the bullets, but was still standing when the three agents ran out of ammunition.

Her beautiful face was still visible, but her body was halfway between a woman's and something amorphous, slimy, and tentacled. Out of her head, where her hair had been, tentacles were emerging. Rivulets of green ooze were streaming from the many wounds. Mostyn could already feel a certain paralysis setting in. He turned around, ejected the magazine from his pistol, slammed a new one home, and racked the slide. He grabbed his mirror, held it up, and opened fire, watching the monster in the mirror. The first half dozen bullets missed. The next two, however, smashed their way through the thing's neck, nearly severing the head.

The Gorgon collapsed to the floor. Jones shook himself, muttering, "What the hell?"

NicAskill shook her head and took a deep breath. "My God, I couldn't breathe."

"You two okay?" Mostyn asked.

"Yep," Jones said. "Although for a moment there, it was like I couldn't make a decision."

"Me, too. But I'm ready to go, sir," NicAskill added.

"Where's Dr. Stoppen?" Mostyn asked.

"Here." Stoppen crept around the curve.

"What the hell, Doc?" Jones said. "You holding out on us?"

"No, I wasn't, Jones," Stoppen replied. "When I got here, Mostyn had his mirror out and was shooting at the Gorgon. I thought it best to stay out of the way. After all, I am a librarian first. Not a trained killer."

"Yeah, right," Jones said.

"Okay you two, that's enough," Mostyn said, "let's go. One monster down, one to go."

Down the tunnel they continued, coming out in the auditorium, which smelled of scorched stone from the thermobaric grenade.

Jones swept the place with his flashlight and helmet lamp. "No one alive seems to be here." He pointed at several charred bodies. "Those guys aren't in any position to stop us."

"You do have a knack for the obvious, Jonesy," NicAskill said.

"Just sayin'," Jones replied.

"Enough!" Mostyn's voice was not loud, but it was firm. "The masked man disappeared when I tossed the stun grenade on the dais," Mostyn said. "There must be another tunnel somewhere around there with a concealed entrance."

The team walked to the dais and Jones swept the area with the twin beams of his lights.

"Give me your flashlight," Mostyn said.

Jones handed the light to him, and Mostyn walked to the back wall, sweeping the beam of light across the stones that made up the wall. Not finding what he was looking for, he panned the beam of light across the floor.

"Ah, here it is," he said, pointing to a crack along a portion of the line where the floor and wall met. "That shouldn't be there. It should be mortared like the rest of the wall."

Mostyn then played the beam of light along the wall, spying out the faint lines of a door. "I don't see a trigger, unless…" He pushed and the door swung inwards, revealing another tunnel.

Stepping into the opening, he turned to Jones. "Wedge this open so Baker and Hammerschmidt can follow." He motioned for NicAskill and Stoppen to follow him.

Jones called out on entering the tunnel, "I saw Baker and Hammerschmidt enter the auditorium with Kemper when I jammed open the door."

Mostyn waved his hand to signal he'd heard.

The tunnel was well lit and they crept along, ready for action. It made a couple right angle turns and finally emptied into a large chamber. A chamber that was brightly illuminated and filled with books, thousands of books sitting on the shelves that reached from the floor to the ceiling along all four walls. In the middle was a large desk and chair. In one corner was a large and ornate Oriental folding screen. The screen was black and on it was a swirling chaos of red and orange, with two yellow cat eyes peering out of the chaos.

From around the screen, stepped the masked man. "You have found me. Most unfortunate for you."

Mostyn raised his pistol.

"You cannot kill me, Mr. Mostyn," the masked man said, raising his hand.

"Want to see me try?" Mostyn replied.

"Many men have, you see, and I am still here. However, while *I* remain *you* and *your team* will simply disappear. And when the moon is once again right for the ceremony, I'll sacrifice Dr. Kemper and Agent NicAskill to open the gate and usher in this universe's night."

Mostyn pulled the trigger. The bullet stopped inches away from the masked man's raised hand and fell to the floor.

"Holy shit!" Jones muttered.

Behind Mostyn, Jones, and NicAskill, Dr. Stoppen took out of his pocket a small black object and tossed it over Jones's head. The little thing hit the floor, bounced once, and transformed into a hulking black monstrosity.

The masked man cried out, reached into his sleeve, withdrew his hand, and threw a handful of red dust into the air. While turning to flee, however, the monstrosity reached out, grabbed and pulled the screaming man to itself, and vanished.

"What the hell was that?" Jones asked.

"A class three demidaimonus," Stoppen said. "A gift from Dr. Bardon. For emergency use only."

"Well, I'll be damned," NicAskill said. "And you had this thing all the time?"

"Well, not all the time," Stoppen replied. "Dr. Bardon gave it to me before he left. He thought we might have use for it. But only in the most dire emergency. I thought this qualified."

Mostyn had a frown on his face. "Why you and not me?"

"Dr. Bardon said the demidaimonus was only to be used to secure the book and nothing else."

"I see," Mostyn replied.

"Why didn't you tell us?" Jones asked.

"Because Bardon said not to. If you have an issue with him swearing me to secrecy, take it up with him."

"Don't worry about it, Otto, we're just sayin'," Baker said, having entered the room with Hammerschmidt and Kemper at the tail end of the conversation. "We all know Bardon moves in mysterious ways his wonders to perform."

Mostyn clapped Jones on the shoulder. "You ought to know by now, the Director has lots of goodies up his sleeves. Just wish he would have let me know about this one."

"What I don't get," Jones said, "is why he just doesn't do all this himself instead of sending us in harm's way."

Mostyn let out a laugh. "Well, Jones, he's not God."

"He's almost like God," NicAskill said. "Are you sure he isn't some kind of supernatural being?"

Mostyn shrugged. "I only know what he told me."

"Which was?" NicAskill prompted.

"That he's human. All too human."

Jones shook his head. "Yeah, right."

EPILOGUE

DR. RAFE BARDON lit his old bent bulldog briar pipe. The scent of sweet Virginia pipe tobacco filled his office. Sitting on the other side of his desk were Mostyn and his team. There was an empty chair in remembrance of Dr. Winifred Petrie.

"I want to begin by saying thank you for an outstanding job. You destroyed a star vampire and the Gorgon, Wing Lee is no longer with us, and his incredible library is being cataloged by Dr. Stoppen. In addition, we have made contact with the lizard people. All in all, a superb job. Thank you all."

"What about the family of Fiorella Flores-Hernandez?" NicAskill asked.

"Yes, very unfortunate," Bardon said, nodding his head slowly and gravely. "They will be adequately taken care of."

"But what did you tell them?" NicAskill pressed.

"Something they could believe," Bardon replied. "After all, who would believe that an extra-dimensional entity killed their daughter by turning her to stone? Why such things are the stuff of myth!" Bardon's face was serious, but there was definitely a twinkle in his eye."

NicAskill continued. "And what happened to Cortado and Salzman?"

"Ah, yes," Bardon said, rubbing his hands together. "It seems they've disappeared."

"You mean they got away?" Jones said.

"Oh, no," Bardon replied. "I mean they disappeared as in they've vanished from public view. While the world at large has two more missing persons, we know they are, for now, safe and sound. They are guests of the US government, and reside in one of our secret facilities."

"Glad I never went into art," Dotty said.

"Indeed, Dr. Kemper, who knew it could be such a dangerous profession. Well, again, I want to thank you for your service. You all did fine work. Thank you."

Bardon stood and everyone knew the meeting was over. As people began filing out, he said, "Mr. Mostyn and Dr. Kemper, if you'd be so kind as to wait a few moments?"

When everyone was gone, Mostyn and Kemper resumed their seats. Dr. Bardon sat and relit his pipe. When he had it going, he spoke.

"I'm glad you got there in time, Pierce, otherwise our Dr. Kemper would not be here and, well, we'd have a bigger problem on our hands."

"What problem, sir?" Dotty asked.

"Don't have time to go into it now, my dear. No, no time."

Mostyn looked at Dotty. "Yes, we were very lucky getting there when we did, sir," Mostyn said.

Bardon smiled. "Oh, I don't think luck had anything to do with it."

"What do you mean, sir?" Mostyn asked.

"Just what I said, my boy, just what I said. Now, unfortunately, I can't give you two any time off. A very big discovery has been made by one of our satellites. The photographs are phenomenal, and I have to send you two out right away."

Bardon slid a folder to the edge of his desk. Mostyn picked up the folder and took a look inside.

"Is this for real?" Mostyn asked.

"It is, Pierce, my boy, it is." Bardon rubbed his hands together in obvious glee. "The opportunity of a lifetime."

"For crying out loud," Dotty said, "will you two let me in on what's going on?"

"Sorry, Dot," Mostyn said, "we're going to Saudi Arabia." A wicked smile appeared on Mostyn's face. "And just think…"

"What?" Dotty said.

"There won't be any trees."

A look of disgust appeared on her face. "Maybe not, but there will be plenty of goddamn sand. For once, just once, I'd like to get an assignment in a city."

Dr. Bardon leaned back in his chair and folded his hands across his ample stomach. Around his pipe, his mouth was stretched in a big smile. "Oh, you will, Dr. Kemper, you will."

A WORD FROM CW

I hope you enjoyed *The Medusa Ritual.*

If you did, please leave a review where you bought the book and on your favorite social media sites. Your review is like word of mouth advertising. And it is pure gold.

Enter my World

Enter my world. A world of terror on a cosmic scale. Just click, tap, or scan the QR code below.

Fear is the most primal of human emotions. And fear of the unknown is the most terrifying of all fears.

If you are new to the Pierce Mostyn Paranormal Investigations series, then *The Medusa Ritual* is an excellent entry point into the series and into my world.

In addition to my Pierce Mostyn Paranormal Investigations books, I've written short stories set in the world of the macabre and arcane. Many of which are only available to folks on my mailing list.

So just click, tap, or scan the QR code to enter my world of terror and the macabre. You will get a free copy of *The Feeder* and you'll get my monthly email of news and curated contact. Terror awaits!

CONTINUE THE ADVENTURE!

The paranormal investigations of Pierce Mostyn continue in *Demons in the Dunes*. Where some things are better left lost.

Special Agent in Charge Pierce Mostyn and his team have five days to learn an ancient ruin's secrets. Can they do so and survive the ruin's horrors?

When the sandstorm of the century uncovers the lost city of Iram in the heart of Saudi Arabia's Empty Quarter, Dr. Rafe Bardon, Director of the ultra-secret Office of Unidentified Phenomena, sends in his best people to discover if Iram is an active gateway for the nefarious Great Old Ones.

Mostyn and his team, while conducting their archaeological dig, accidentally unleash an ancient horror, which promptly kills one of the members, and reveals that the gateway is still open. And when Dr. Dotty Kemper and her colleagues decide to remove a mummy from its eons-old crypt, the doors to Hell are thrown wide open.

Against hordes of the living dead, Mostyn and his team are forced into a losing battle as they attempt to survive Iram's secrets. Will Dr. Bardon's rescue effort be in time to not only save Mostyn, but seal the gateway and stop the Great Old Ones?

Demons in the Dunes is the sixth book in CW Hawes's Pierce Mostyn Paranormal Investigations series.

If you love weird fiction, horror, monsters, humor, thrilling action, and the Cthulhu Mythos, get in on Pierce Mostyn's adventure today — if you dare!

Demons in the Dunes is available at your favorite online store. Check it out! Just click, tap, or scan the QR code.

BOOKS BY CW HAWES

CW is a multi-genre author.

The books below are portals to his many exciting worlds. And no AI was used in the writing of these books. Books by a human for a human.

Pierce Mostyn Paranormal Investigations

The X-Files meets Cthulhu. Pierce Mostyn does battle with inter-dimensional monsters bent on the destruction of humanity.

Nightmare in Agate Bay
Stairway to Hell
Terror in the Shadows
Van Dyne's Vampires
The Medusa Ritual
Demons in the Dunes
Van Dyne's Zuvembies

In the Shadow of the Mountains of Madness

Justinia Wright Private Investigator Mysteries

Justinia Wright is the PI with panache. These slow burn mysteries, written in homage to Rex Stout's Nero Wolfe, are sure to satisfy your craving for intriguing puzzles, quirky characters, and wise-cracking humor.

Vampire House and Other Early Cases of Justinia Wright, PI
Festival of Death
Trio in Death-Sharp Minor
But Jesus Never Wept
The Conspiracy Game
A Nest of Spies
When Friends Must Die
Death Makes a House Call
To Right a Wrong
The Nine Deadly Dolls
Ripples on the Pond
Christmas with the Wrights
Minneapolis's Finest
Jack in the Box
Sauerkraut Days
Justinia Wright Private Investigator Omnibus Edition

Magnolia Bluff Crime Chronicles

Tense slow burn mysteries set in our favorite town in the Texas Hill Country.

Death Wears a Crimson Hat

Ten Million Ways to Die
Who Mourns Elektra?
Death by Moonlight

The Rocheport Saga

A post-apocalyptic adventure series in the style of cozy catastrophes such as *Earth Abides* and *Day of the Triffids*. Join Bill Arthur as he strives to build a new and better world on the ashes of the old.

The Morning Star
The Shining City
The Divided City
The Troubled City
By Leaps and Bounds
Freedom's Freehold
Take to the Sky

Decopunk

Alternative history adventures in a world where World War II never happened and swing is still king.

From the Files of Lady Dru Drummond
The Moscow Affair
The Golden Fleece Affair

Rand Hart Adventures
Rand Hart and the Pajama Putsch

Tales of the Macabre

For the horror lover in you.
    Do One Thing For Me
    Metamorphosis
    What the Next Day Brings
    Ancient History

Anthologies

Enjoy CW's stories in these short story collections.
    The Phantom Games
    Beyond the Sea
    Overmorrow
    Arachnapocalypse! The Anthology
    Once Upon a WolfPack

Available at your favorite online retailer. Just click, tap, or scan the QR code to be taken to My Books page for the links!

ABOUT CW HAWES

CW Hawes has written over 50 novels and shorter works of fiction. He was also an award-winning poet and had over 200 poems appear in ezines and and print.

He is a founding member of the Underground Authors and was the impetus for the highly successful Magnolia Bluff Crime Chronicles series.

After 35 years of working in county government, he retired at the beginning of 2015 and began a second career as a fictioneer. Perhaps some of the horrors Pierce Mostyn faces can be traced to his creator's own experiences in county government and beyond. Perhaps.

CW lives in Southern California. He enjoys reading, writing, chess and other board games, his daily morning walk, and contemplating the meaning of life while smoking his pipe. He also hasn't met a doughnut or a pizza he doesn't like, is something of a tea snob, and rocks out to Handel and Vaughan Williams.

You can get curated content and the occasional free story

when you join his mailing list, and you can reach him at his website, on X, and also Facebook.

To join his mailing list, click, tap, or scan the QR code:

To visit him on his website, click, tap, or scan the QR code:

To visit him on X, click, tap, or scan the QR code:

To visit him on Facebook, click, tap, or scan the QR code: